Repo man

m a x

New York Times Bestselling Author

m o n r o e

Dedication

To dumb choices for the right reasons.
(If you've been there, you get it.)

Repo man

Prologue

THE VAMPIRE WITH THE GREEN EYES IS THE HANDsomest one.

Obviously. *Duh.*

He's not the tallest one in my new doll set—that one has dark hair and a scar painted across his cheek like he's a scary fighter or something—but he's the one I like best. His hair is a soft yellowish color, and his eyes are a funny kind of green that look kind of purple if you tilt him just right.

I like to tilt him *a lot.*

I am nine years old today, which means I'm officially old enough to stay up later than my little sister Bonnie and pick my own cake. I like strawberry with vanilla buttercream. It's the best cake in the whole wide world.

Mommy and Daddy gave me this doll set during my birthday party this afternoon. It was a big party—more big than last year—with lots of my mommy and daddy's friends. And very important people too. At least, that's what my mommy told me. She said some of Daddy's important businesspeople came to celebrate with me because I'm such a special girl.

And I like when Daddy's important people come because they always bring the biggest, most fancy gifts.

I wore a pretty pink dress and white shiny shoes. My mommy said my dress costed a lot of moneys and that she got it at a really fancy store. I think it's called Channel? I don't know, but it's my mommy's favorite store.

Anyway, my party was huge, and I got to open so many gifts.

My daddy is an important businessman. I don't know what his business is, but my mommy says it's very important. My mommy doesn't have a job, but she's too busy to have a job. That's why me and my baby sister Bonnie spend so much time with our nanny Celeste.

My nanny Celeste is the best. She's—

I hear footsteps near my door.

Oh no! I'm supposed to be asleep!

I dive under my blankets and pretend I'm sleeping.

And I wait and wait and wait there under my blankets until my warm breath starts to make me all itchy and sweaty.

But when Mommy or Daddy or Nanny Celeste doesn't knock on my door, I push my blankets off my face and let out a big, deep breath. *Holy moly, it was getting hot under there.*

I turn on my night-light by my bed and sit up again.

And I line my vampire dolls back up so I can look at them all.

Yep. The vampire doll with the green eyes is definitely the most handsome.

He's my favorite.

I pick him up and hold him in my right hand, and then I pick up the human girl doll with "Blair" embroidered on the dress in pretty pink letters with my left. Blair is my name, and this doll is supposed to be me. My Blair doll's dress is white but also kind of yellowish. I think my mommy calls the color creamy.

It reminds me of a dress Mommy keeps in her closet in a big box with tissue paper all around it. It's the dress she wore when she married Daddy.

I press the doll's faces close together. "You've been chosen," I say in my deepest, most serious voice, making the vampire doll talk.

The Blair doll gasps. I make her gasp. "Chosen?" I make her whisper.

"Yes," I answer for him. "Your mommy and daddy said you're a special girl."

"Why am I special?"

"Because of your blood."

My mommy told me that I'm getting old enough now to learn more big-girl things, and that was one of the things she told me when she was talking to me about secret stuff I'm not supposed to talk about.

But I have blood inside my body. Every human does. But my blood is good blood. Vampires like my blood a lot. It makes me special.

Mommy says they found out about my blood when I was a baby. And some of my daddy's most important friends know about it too.

Good blood is a very special gift, my mommy says.

My daddy and my mommy aren't vampires. They're humans like me. But my mommy says that I am so special because of my special blood that I will be chosen by one of the most important, strongest, most special vampire boys when I'm a grown-up girl.

I make the vampire doll stand taller than the girl.

"I will take care of you," I say for him.

"Do you love me?" my Blair doll asks.

"Yes, I love you. You're a special girl."

I wish I could tell my best friend Laura about my vampire dolls and my special blood, but my mommy and daddy said that Laura's family doesn't know the secret. Not many human families know about the special blood and special vampires.

I'm not allowed to talk about any of it at school. Or at church. Or anywhere, really. And I only ever hear my parents talk about it when certain people are at our house. Only humans who know. And vampires too. Sometimes my mommy and daddy have special vampires at our house. They're big, strong men and they're kind of scary, but I think that's just because they're so strong.

"I won't tell anyone about the secret," my Blair doll says to the vampire doll.

"Good. You're a good special girl," the vampire doll says.

"And you love me?"

"And I love you."

I set the vampire doll down and smooth the Blair doll's hair down her back. "You don't have to worry," I tell her. "A vampire will choose you. Because you have the special blood."

My mommy says when I'm a grown-up girl, I'll go to secret

special events and a vampire man will choose me because he loves me and my special blood.

"They'll feel it," Mommy told me. "And you will too."

I pick my favorite vampire doll back up, the blond one with the green-but-sometimes-purple eyes and examine his face closer.

"When I grow up and get chosen," I whisper. "I hope it's someone like you."

1

KANE

*I*F THIS WERE A NORMAL PARTY, I'D BE ENJOYING myself.

I'd work the room, make people laugh their asses off, and probably convince at least three total strangers they've known me for years. I'd flirt a little with the bartender in the name of getting her to employ longer pours and talk the host into letting us fuck around with karaoke rather than listen to this fancy classical shit.

I bring golden-retriever-with-a-knife energy.

I'm charming as shit and excellent at making friends, but if someone starts trouble, I won't hesitate to be the one to end it—*or them.*

But this isn't a normal party, and tonight, I can't be myself at all.

Tonight, I'm background noise.

Tonight, I'm a nobody in a mask.

Being invisible is *not* my natural state, but if I let even ten percent of my personality out in this room, someone would notice. And if someone notices, someone dies.

Real talk, my brother Cal and I should *not* be here. Naturally, that means it was mostly my idea, and the purpose of our mission is to find out how far up shit's creek we are.

Very early this morning, my brothers and I may have made a *slightly controversial* decision involving the elites—by killing three of their gofers in Kylie Moon's driveway and kidnapping her.

Technically, we *rescued* her. Though, I'm guessing the elites won't be interested in that particular distinction since they're the villains in our scenario.

But Kylie Moon doesn't belong to the elites; she belongs to my elder brother, Rook. They're fated. Written in the fucking stars. Which means right now he's holed up somewhere safe with her, probably basking in the glow of what happens when destiny finally stops dragging its feet and gets naked.

Lucky bastard.

Meanwhile, Cal and I are standing in the middle of a ballroom full of elite vampires who would happily rip our heads off if they knew who we were.

Rook doesn't know we're *here* here, though, and he wouldn't like it if he did. He thinks we're running surveillance from a *safe* distance. He doesn't have a clue we walked straight into the viper's den.

I adjust my mask and give my best impression of an apathetic *GQ* model in a tuxedo.

Across the ballroom, my brother Cal stands like a marble statue, pretending not to hear every heartbeat in the room. He's the youngest of us three Slater brothers, and I swear, his hearing is supernatural even by vampire standards. Most vampires can hear things humans can't, but Cal could hear a squirrel fart three counties over if he focused hard enough.

"Tell me again why I didn't draw the straw for the brother who gets to stay with the girl?" I tease, murmuring so quietly, I'm basically just moving my lips.

Cal glances up, meeting my eyes, and the look on his face says, *Stop being such an annoying fuck right now.*

This is what I'm talking about. The Avengers would kill for hearing like his.

Chastised, I fade into the background as much as I can, and it's clear by the way Cal is basically standing between two lush potted plants across the ballroom, he's doing the same.

This event is being held in the kind of decadent mansion most people only see in movies, and it's located in one of the most opulent areas in Boston. Lit chandeliers are hanging from the extraordinarily tall ceilings, marble covering every square foot of floor, and a string quartet of men in tuxedos plays classical music in a ballroom that sits past the opulent staircase that's showcased near the entrance.

People are dressed to impress. The men are all wearing sleek suits or tuxedos, and the women are in formal gowns. Masks cover the men's faces, but the women's are on full display.

Predator and unknowing prey is clearly the vibe here.

Pretentious, evil fucks.

The entire scene bleeds arrogance that only comes with generational money and a complete lack of fear. Every man in this room holds power, and clearly, believes he's untouchable. But that's because the world has always bent the knee for every single bastard standing in this room.

Even if most humans don't know that vampires exist, the vampire elite have always been something to fear.

Though, I can't deny the masks are tasteful. They don't showcase feathers or sequins or gawdy bullshit. They're just sleek black lacquer over bone-white and shaped to each male face with perfection. Cal and I managed to snag two off a table when we snuck in through a back-door entrance, blending in despite the fact that we'd never have been invited, even if we hadn't killed some of their friends.

My brothers and I are not elite vampires by any stretch of the imagination. In fact, the elite believe we're beneath them, lower-class scum under their shiny shoes. Blue-collar-ant-worker bitches who do all the dirty work that keeps society moving.

To them, I'm a scrub. A lowly twenty-seven-year-old vampire who works a blue-collar job as a repo man. They see my brothers—Rook is a garbage man, and Cal is a mechanic and does demolition work—as the same.

Frankly, it's a tale as old as time. Our genetics might be otherworldly like theirs, but our lineage doesn't stem from the "right" bloodlines.

I read the room. An outsider to this situation—someone who isn't aware of vampire elites and how they secretly rule and hold power in a human world—wouldn't know the truth about why this event is happening. They'd probably think it's a fancy masquerade ball for billionaires or some shit, but they'd be missing a huge piece of the depraved puzzle.

Because while the bottomless pit of behaviors of men seeking power is the same for vampires as it is for humans, my kind takes it to another level. Women are merchandise to be bought, sold, and *used*. And the human corporations involved are just another pawn.

In my periphery, I see Holland Thorne drift toward the staircase. He's in a black tuxedo with a mask like mine, and his posture is smooth and confident. He's not one of the elites—he's a gofer for them, a fucking errand man—but he moves like someone who desperately wants to be part of their club.

He's the one Cal and I followed here. We've known him for years, mostly from playing hockey against each other in a rec league in Concordia, and he's been a real piece of shit the whole time. But it's only lately that he upped his dickheadedness exponentially.

Kylie Moon was his assignment—a human woman with the highly coveted *blood of the three*—and my brother Rook's fated mate. Holland was supposed to lure her into this world without her even knowing what she signed up for, subsequently stealing her right out from under a Slater brother's nose and leaving us to deal with Rook's broken ass.

If it weren't for our extreme measures, she'd be here tonight. Holland Thorne would no doubt be parading her around the room so the elites could decide how much she's worth. But instead, she's with Rook in an undisclosed location in Worcester.

My brother knew Kylie was his the instant he turned the magic number twenty-eight—an important year in all male vampires' lives. It's the year the aging process slows down to about a fifth of a normal human. But more importantly, it's the year you lock in on your beloved and are capable of feeling *the bond*. It's when destiny helps you find *her*.

But the elites' bullshit games have destroyed most fated mate bonds from ever occurring. They've spent the last century using their mighty influence to keep all the human women with the *blood of the three* to themselves—because it gives them all the power and control—and sending the rest of the balance all out of whack.

It used to be *the blood of four*, but one bloodline has already perished because of what the elites do.

Holland Thorne stinks up the room with his fake smiles and try-hard laughs as I look on from the shadows, and my impatience rears its ugly head. I swear, he's such a slimy fucking prick. I reach my hand into the pocket of my dress slacks and grip the handle of my knife.

If I didn't know I would be writing my own death sentence, I'd kill Holland myself, right here, right now.

I sigh and let go of the knife.

Surface-level, this event probably seems harmless, but that's because it's merely a preview for the real event. Soon, there will be an actual auction in New York where most of the women in this room will be sold off to the highest bidder.

The women circulate and smile and wave and giggle and flirt, while the men observe them.

It's a slaughterhouse in silk gloves.

I can't avoid the intention that seeps from the male attendees' postures and movements and minds. I can't read their minds, but I can sense their intentions—what they want, what they're planning to do, and what their motivations stem from. It's a gift—just like Cal's hearing and Rook's telepathy. I've always had this power, and it's served me well, for the most part. But in a room like this, my mind is being throttled with disgusting selfishness, and, in most cases, downright evil intentions over and over.

Each man behind the mask, each elite vampire licking his lips over the females on display, is not here for love or romance. They are here to look at the inventory. And yes, that's exactly what these women are to them—inventory.

Some have the *blood of the three*, and those are the most important to the elites. They give them the most power and the most pleasure, and they're the only ones they can breed.

But they also just want human women with beauty and intelligence and whatever something special attracts the elites' eyes. They can't breed them because they don't have the right bloodline, but they'll use them in the name of keeping all the best for themselves.

Because that's all these women are to them. Something to *own*. Something to *use*.

And trust me, what they do with that ownership is a thousand times worse than anyone can imagine.

Cal is still across the room, and because it's who I am, I can't stop myself from fucking with him a little.

"It'd be a damn shame if I died tonight, you know? Have you seen how good I look in this tux?" My words are almost inaudible, but from across the room, I don't miss the way Cal rolls his eyes beneath his mask.

I take that as a good sign that he's still relaxed. I'm relying on his ears to pinpoint any instant danger. If he's still capable of getting annoyed with me, then we're not seconds away from being dismembered.

When I say we shouldn't be here, I really fucking mean it.

Our names are being dragged through the mud as we speak. I have no doubt a witch-hunt is already being organized to track us down and kill us, and all the people who want that to happen are in this room.

Because we took Kylie Moon.

But sometimes it's better to hide in plain sight. No doubt, this is the last fucking place they'd expect Cal and me to be. And with their current focused intentions—their minds and eyes and dicks fixated on the women—they're not thinking about the three Slater brothers they still need to kill.

They're probably saving that for later—a problem for tomorrow.

An older but very imposing man with pepper-gray hair and dressed in a sleek black suit walks past me, and for the briefest of moments, we make eye contact. His eyes are this bright, almost glowing, green, but I stay neutral and don't let myself be the first one to look away. *Looking away shows weakness. Looking away is suspicious.* It's a risk, making eye contact like this, because depending on this man's powers, he might be able to see inside my head or read my mind or know I have a knife in my pocket that I'm prepared to use.

Eventually, though, he looks past me, a faint smile cresting his lips, and he crosses the room for a destination unknown. I don't know him personally, but I know he's an elite vamp. A very old, very rich, very influential one. I can see it in his eyes. I can smell it emanating from his skin. And I know he's at least a shield like Holland Thorne because I can't read his intentions at all.

Another elite vampire—much younger than the first—moves past me, just barely brushing my shoulder. But he doesn't notice me at all because his eyes are too hooked on a blond woman across the room. My mind works to see if I can read *his* intentions.

Breed. Drain. Use up.

My skin fucking crawls.

In a room like this, it's easy to read intention because *predatory* interest is different from desire or love or something that's good. The mind whispers it efficiently and without complications. Predatory intentions aren't clogged with overthinking or loose ends of doubts. They're just there, clear and precise.

Fuck. I think I've had enough of this shit.

I meander over toward Cal, hoping he's managed to listen in on enough conversations that we can get out of here, but something tugs at me.

It's not physical or visual, but there's a *pull*. It's subtle at first, but then it becomes sharp enough that I feel it in my chest, and my feet falter back two steps.

Cal meets my eyes from across the room, and I can tell by the way his blue eyes turn down beneath his mask, he's confused.

Trust me, bro. I'm fucking confused.

Paranoia starts to flow into my veins. *Is this some kind of mind control? Have we been sniffed out?*

All the while, the pull keeps intensifying. It feels like someone tied a line to my sternum from across the room and is yanking as hard as they can.

My eyes follow the invisible string.

And that's when I see *her.*

Dark hair that's not black or brown but something in between falls in smooth waves down her back. Her blue eyes are clear and bright and almost glacial under the chandelier lights.

She's standing near the base of the staircase, next to a large marble statue, and her posture only showcases grace. She's downright beautiful as she laughs at something a man behind a mask whispers to her.

The pull tightens so hard my hand goes to my chest. *Fuck me.*

"Kane." My brother Cal's voice is in my ear. He's closer now, but I can't even look at him.

Because I'm not really here.

Because the second I saw her, something inside me locked.

It's not attraction or curiosity. It's *need*—for survival. Like every fucked-up cell in my vampire body has decided it will revolve around her for the rest of my fucking life.

Mine.

The room dulls. The music fades into static. And all the while, she hasn't looked at me a single time. But she doesn't need to. This thing—the thing that's happening to me—doesn't require eye contact. It only requires proximity.

She turns slightly, stepping away from one of the masked men, and the movement drags my attention with it like gravity just rewrote itself.

Cal steps in front of my line of sight deliberately. "Hey," he says quietly. "What are you doing?"

"Appreciating the art."

"There's no fucking art on that side of the room."

My quiet laugh comes out thin.

Cal tries to search my eyes because I'm probably acting like a total dumb fuck right now, but the pull just keeps growing stronger the more I look at her.

And that's when it clicks—she's here, at this preview, with the vampire elite.

She's a part of it.

And she doesn't look afraid. She looks…excited and proud. She *is* excited and proud. Her intentions stem from believing this is her purpose. She believes this is her version of a fairy tale.

She thinks this is a good thing.

She takes a few steps, and the magnetic force between us snaps tighter.

I can't look away.

For the first time in my life, I understand exactly what Rook meant when he said it was immediate.

I know, without a doubt, that I am absolutely, undeniably, catastrophically screwed.

Because it's *her*.

And I've found her in the middle of an event surrounded by elite vampires who want to kill me, and not only does she naïvely want to be here—want to be fucking mated to an elite vampire— she doesn't even know I exist.

2

BLAIR

ONIGHT, I'M MEANT TO BE *SEEN*.

The mansion is enormous, and that's saying something coming from a girl like me, because my parents' estate in Boston is the kind of place people drool over. This place is so big and extravagant it somehow makes the fifteen-thousand-square-foot house I grew up in look like a starter home.

I've been to fancy parties—I've even attended red-carpet events—but I've never in my life been to something like *this*.

Marble floors gleam beneath the light of the chandeliers that drip with crystals the size of grapes, and glass display cases that would normally hold priceless sculptures now hold rows of champagne flutes instead. A string quartet provides the ambiance, while masked men move easily through the room in perfectly tailored suits.

And *wow*. Masks or not, it's obvious these men didn't get powerful by skipping the gym. Most of them are tall with broad shoulders and confident in that quiet way men get when they have a lot of money and power.

One of these men might choose me.

I catch my reflection in a darkened window and smooth a hand down the fabric of my dress. It's cream and silk and took my mother and me hours to find during a shopping trip—for this very event—in New York.

I can't believe it's finally happening.

My hair and makeup are still intact, and just the right amount of cleavage peeks out from the neckline of my dress. Though, across the room, another girl in a red dress is making a much more *aggressive* cleavage presentation choice.

I swear, if she leans forward by just an inch, we're all going to get a nipple shot.

Beautiful and sexy but not obscene, my mom would say.

I straighten my shoulders and look back toward the masked men moving through the room.

These men hold all the power and money and wealth in the world. And soon, one of them will hold all my dreams and my future.

One of them will choose me to be his.

My pulse thrums in excitement. I feel like I've been waiting all twenty-three years of my life for this moment. Hell, I've been preparing for it since before I knew how to tie my own shoes.

From a young age, I've known the truth about vampires. Not the cartoon or movie versions, but the *real* ones. The royal elites. The ones who aren't showcased in the headlines but are so powerful behind the scenes they shape entire cities. My father says they control economies and foreign trade and industries across the globe.

My bloodline was confirmed when I was a baby.

"Rare," my mom used to say while brushing my hair before school. "And special. That's you."

I am one of the lucky ones—one of *the blood of the three*. It's Windsor blood, from my daddy's side, and both my little sister Bonnie and I have it. But out of us Windsor girls, *I* am the next generation to be chosen. The last Windsor woman who was chosen by an elite vampire was my father's great-aunt Estelle.

This isn't white-picket fences and minivans. This is royalty. This is fairy tales. And I'm the next lucky Windsor woman who is destined to be inside this world and live a life that's bigger than most girls could ever dream.

At this event, there are a lot of women, but not all of them carry the same bloodline as me. I have one of only three bloodlines in the world that can marry and have children with a vampire.

It wasn't always easy growing up in a human-focused world where you never spoke about *this* world or the existence of vampires and bloodlines. This isn't something I could talk about at school or with girlfriends or college dorm roommates.

Only those in the inner circle are allowed to know.

And tonight, everyone in this room *knows*.

It's a relief, but it's also a competition. There are formidable women here—some almost as beautiful as me—and my purpose is to catch the eye of my future vampire husband.

"Would you like a drink?" A masked man with chocolate-brown hair offers me a flute of champagne. His voice showcases this deep vibrato that I feel inside my chest. His eyes are a dark navy that almost looks onyx beneath the soft glow of the room, and they linger on me for a fraction longer than most would consider polite, but I understand. Anticipation is high for both of us.

"Yes." I smile, but not too wide or excited. Just…confident. "Thank you." I lift the glass to my lips, never letting my gaze stray from his. I can't even begin to tell you how many times my mother made me practice exact scenarios like this in our kitchen.

In order to get the best, you need to be the best, my mom would say.

"What's your name?" he asks.

"Blair Windsor." I purposefully lick a drop of champagne off my top lip. I don't ask him his name. I know the rules. They'll tell you if they want to tell you. That's how it works.

"You're beautiful, Blair," he says, reaching out to gently brush a few strands of hair off my shoulders, just barely missing my skin. They aren't supposed to touch me until they claim me—it's one of the highest rules of order for the whole selection process.

"Thank you."

"I'm Damien. Damien Snow."

The little girl inside me is squealing that he just told me his *full* name, but I keep her on the down-low and respond confidently. "It's a pleasure, Damien."

His lips press into each other, and I imagine him pressing his lips to my skin. "It certainly is a pleasure, Blair. A very exciting pleasure."

I smile again. And I take another drink from my glass of champagne. The bubbles pop and fizz in my throat, and I play the role of being interested but not too interested. Men like

Damien can smell desperation from a hundred miles away. My mother taught me that. She told me they can sense insecurity and doubt, and they know when a woman isn't confident.

They don't want to choose a girl with poor self-esteem, she'd say. *They want beauty and elegance and poise.*

I let the silence linger between Damien and me. Occasionally making eyes at him over my glass of champagne. I relish the moments when he rakes his eyes over me, taking in my hair and my face and the curve of my breasts.

And I give him the space to do it, sometimes letting my eyes move over the room as I take sips from my champagne.

Some of the girls here I don't recognize at all, but some I've known since childhood, and we grew up in the same inner circles.

I'm surprised that a few of the girls look outwardly nervous. *Amateurs. You never let them smell nerves.* Did their moms not tell them confidence is currency like mine did?

I honestly don't know, but I only see it as an advantage. Sure, I can't deny I feel tiny swarms of butterflies flitting about my belly, but I will *not* let anyone see it.

Damien doesn't speak much. He doesn't try to engage me in small talk or ask me a lot of questions about myself. But so far, I'm finding that none of the men really do. That probably comes later, you know?

Eventually, when he excuses himself with a promise of seeing each other again, I move toward the base of the staircase, silently reminding myself to keep my chin lifted and my shoulders relaxed.

Be calm. Be confident. Be worth the attention.

Someone laughs abruptly near my shoulder, damn near startling me off my game, but I quickly pull myself together.

But when I let myself observe the room, my attention is straight up held hostage by a man wearing a black tuxedo. His green eyes sit beneath a black mask like the others, his hair is a gorgeous shade of blond, and his jaw is as sharp as chiseled stone. He's not older, like the silver-haired elites. He's younger, maybe a few years older than me, and incredibly tall, with muscular, broad shoulders and long, strong legs.

He's Adonis-level handsome.

And he's looking directly at me.

Instantly, the air feels heavy between us, and the room narrows as the strangest sensation washes over my body.

My stomach tightens, and I get the sense that I should know him. I feel like I've seen him or met him before, but at the same time, I can't find a single memory in my brain to match.

But then, for one irrational flicker of time, I feel nine years old again, sitting cross-legged on my bed, holding a blond-haired vampire doll in my hands, tilting it toward the window so his eyes looked almost violet in the light.

My fingers tighten around the stem of my glass, and the green-eyed stranger keeps staring at me.

Who is he? And why does he feel so…familiar?

I'm tempted to walk over to him. I'm tempted to go introduce myself and ask him who he is, but that's not how it goes. The women do not seek out the men; it doesn't work like that.

If he wants to talk to me, he has to come to me.

I take a quick swig of champagne and work to regain my composure.

And when Damien returns, asking me if I'd like to meet some of his friends, I follow.

I glide. I flutter my lashes and smile. But I can't stop myself from glancing over my shoulder once more.

Green eyes are still on me.

And I really don't want him to look away.

3

KANE

*S*HE'S LAUGHING.

And that's the part that crushes my fucking soul.

Not the masks or the obscene wealth or the way the elite bloodsuckers exploit these women with their eyes. *Trust me, all of that is pretty fucking awful.* But it's the fact that she's enjoying herself. It's the fact that her laugh is bright and flirtatious and completely devoid of the fear that laugh should hold beneath the surface.

Three elites surround her, taking her in, whispering hushed conversation in her direction. And all she wants to do is entertain them. She wants to play this game. But the saddest part of all is that she thinks the game is fair.

She *thinks* she knows the score.

She tilts her head just enough to give the man with black eyes access to her neck. My blood boils when he leans in and holds his nose just above her skin. He wants to claim her. He wants to possess her. He wants to breed her. He wants to fuck her. He wants to use her blood for his own power and pleasure and selfish desires.

He wants to take every ounce of life and vibrance from her, and he doesn't care if her death would be the cost.

His hungry intentions invade my mind.

Her naïve ignorance breaks my fucking heart.

I want to murder him.

Visions of me striding right over to the vile piece of shit and slicing his throat infiltrate my head, and it takes every ounce of self-control inside me not to follow through.

I can see too much right now. This is the first time in my life that I feel like my gift is a noose around my neck. It's choking. It's clawing. It's fucking suffocating me by the second.

I clench my fists when the two other men lean in to smell her neck too—smell her blood.

Her blood is one of the three. Even I can smell that from here. Hell, every vampire cock within a thousand-mile radius knows what those bloodlines smell like. It's the only one we can breed with, and when you combine it with the fact that she's a virgin—*yeah, I can smell that too*—her body might as well be a biological siren's call.

She smiles and giggles as she gives them access to her skin. But they don't push the line; that's not how these bastards handle shit. They keep the violence and the cruelty for afterward—behind closed doors where no one but them can see.

She is prey, and she has no idea she is currently flitting around the goddamn lion's den. Hell, even fucking lions have dignity. Even lions let their prey know the score. But not these men. They don't want her to know the score. They want her to stay lost in her childlike intentions of fucking fairy tales and a fanged-up prince charming.

That's not how they handle all the women, but it's how they handle women like her. The ones who know. The ones who were raised to believe the lie.

She laughs again, smiling at the vampire with dark eyes and an even darker smile, and my jaw locks so hard my molars grind.

"Relax." Calloway is right beside me right now, but he's pretending to be incredibly interested in a glass of bourbon I know he won't drink while we're here. His voice is a harsh whisper. "Fucking relax."

"I'm fine."

He shakes his head at me. *No, you're not fucking fine*, he's silently saying.

I don't answer, but when I try to drag my eyes away from her, I fucking can't.

The vampire demon's fingers hover over her neck now. He's showing the other two men that he's planning to claim her. He's casual in his action and rule-bound in his distance, but his body language showcases possession. He's also testing her—trying to figure out how fucking pliant she is.

She doesn't balk.

He fucking loves that.

He wants her naïve. I can feel it. I can see it. I can fucking smell it.

And she smiles like she's being admired and complimented and showered with some kind of desired affection. She thinks this is about courtship.

A violent jolt hits every nerve ending inside my body. And the pull, the invisible string that's embedded itself in my chest, tugs tighter. I feel like someone dropped a hook in my spine and has started reeling me across the room—directly to her.

I take one step closer without realizing I've done it, and Cal's hand grasps my shoulder just enough to discreetly yank me back.

"Easy, bro," he whispers. "Fucking rein it in."

"I'm good," I lie.

Black Eyes studies her closely.

Her pulse thrums wildly at her neck, but she's not afraid—I can smell anticipation and excitement.

I flex my fists. My jaw ticks.

"Enough." Calloway's voice drops. "E-fucking-nough."

My brother can tell I'm moments away from losing it. Though he doesn't know why. His intentions are showcasing a need to remove me from the room because of what is happening here—the scene, the system, what this all stands for—but he hasn't noticed her.

He doesn't even know she exists.

But I do.

To me, she's *all* that exists.

I don't look at Cal. I fear if I do, he'll know something has shifted in me. I'm too fucking raw right now, too overcome by the pull, too far gone by her grip on my instincts.

The man's hand skims above her waist, and she doesn't pull away, letting the pulse of an almost touch move through her. If anything, she leans in, willing contact to happen.

And the urge to kill overwhelms me.

Mine.

The word isn't rational, but it's the only word inside my head.

Mine. Mine. Mine.

She shifts slightly, scanning the room for a second. Her eyes pass over the crowd—and land on me. The man leans down to say something low into her ear, and I just start…walking.

Toward them. Toward her.

But I only get a few steps ahead before I feel a strong grip on my arm, pulling me back.

"What the fuck are you doing?" Cal whispers harshly into my ear. He's concerned. He thinks I'm unraveling.

He's probably right.

My eyes are still on her and the other vampire, and when his focus goes back to her throat for another sniff, the urge to murder blurs my vision red.

Cal's definitely right.

Wedding bells and a handsome groom and vampire babies and a big mansion with a happy family are her entire world right now. And all that guy sees is power.

She is so fucking naïve it's killing me.

I want to cross the room, but I know I won't stop at broken bones. I won't stop at anything. I won't stop until heads are literally rolling.

"Leave." Calloway tightens his grip. "Now."

My brother doesn't ask questions, and he doesn't give me any more chances. He steers me down an empty hallway in the mansion and toward an exit out a discreet side door.

And the whole time, behind us, the music swells and conversation chatters and her laugh floats over it all.

The pull doesn't loosen. It only grows tighter.

And every step I take away from her feels like I'm fucking dying.

4

SATURDAY MORNING FEELS LIKE CHAMPAGNE. Not the literal kind—though last night's bubbles are still fizzing somewhere in the back of my throat—but the sensation of it. I feel light and effervescent and like my whole body is freaking sparkling with something bigger than anything I've ever experienced.

I wake up slowly, stretching my arms and legs beneath my cream silk sheets and marshmallow-soft white comforter. I still live at my parents' house. After I graduated from Boston University, I moved back home because, well, being a career woman is not my fate.

My fate will be filled with something far bigger and better than that.

Eeep. I can't wait.

Last night, I felt like I was floating on a freaking cloud. I've never been in a room with that many vampire elites. I can't deny it was a little intimidating at times, but they're, like, some of the most important men in the world. I mean, how could anyone not be a little intimidated by that?

And soon, one of them will be my husband.

Holy hell. I flip over onto my belly and practically squeal into my pillow.

I can't believe it's finally happening.

I sit up and press my palm to my chest as if I can physically hold the feeling in place. The excitement and anticipation are downright intoxicating, and I fear if I let myself breathe too hard, it'll float away.

Or, goodness, maybe *I'll* float away.

Three soft knocks sound at my door. "Blair, honey? You awake?" My mother's voice fills my ears.

"Yeah. You can come in."

Devney Windsor is the kind of woman that can enter a room with such poised calm you'd think it's impossible for her ever to be nervous. It's still morning and she's wearing her silk robe, but her hair is perfect, her makeup already intact, and she has a cup of coffee in her hand.

Her eyes are bright as she walks toward my bed.

"How are you feeling this morning?"

I smile. I can't help it. "Like it's finally happening."

"Oh, my girl. I was hoping you'd say something like that." A small, satisfied smile touches her mouth. "Tell me everything."

"It was exactly like you said it would be." I swing my legs out of bed. "The mansion was insanely beautiful. The event was beyond extravagant. Everything was just…perfect."

"And you held yourself well? Good posture, good smile, and no rambling or asking too many questions?"

"I did everything you said I needed to do," I answer. "I didn't drink too much. I didn't talk too much. I didn't…chase. I let them come to me."

"That's my girl." Her smile consumes her whole face. "And did you meet anyone…interesting?"

I grin. "I met *a lot* of interesting men."

"Oh Blair, I can't deny I'm a little jealous. I've never gotten to experience any of this firsthand, and I just…" She pauses and lets out a dreamy little sigh. "I just can't imagine how incredible it is."

She's not a Windsor by blood; she's a Windsor by marriage. Since she's not one of the *blood of the three* like Bonnie and me, my mother has never been a part of something like this. She's never attended a preview event or the Selection. She only knows about it from what she's been told by Grandma Windsor and other women on my father's side.

When I don't say anything, she reaches out to tap my knee playfully. "Blair, don't leave me hanging, sweetheart! Tell me everything!"

"Okay! Okay!" I laugh. "Well, this man named Damien spoke to me quite a bit," I say, unable to keep the thrill from my voice. "He talked to me longer than anyone else. More than any other girl in the room. I don't know what he does or anything, but I could tell by the way the other men were acting around him he's very important."

"And what's he like?"

"He's…reserved," I say with a shrug. "A little closed off. But I think that's just his style. Like he doesn't use words unless they matter."

"That's usually how powerful men are," my mom hums.

I grin. *My thoughts exactly.*

The door swings open without another knock, and my sister Bonnie strolls in like she owns the whole estate—which, in her mind, she does. Fifteen years old and already armed with a teen-age smirk that could make a grown man flinch.

"Hey, loser! How did the meat market go last night?" She snags something off one of my shelves and flops onto the end of my bed, holding whatever is in her hands against her chest.

But it only takes a moment for me to realize what she's holding.

My doll. My favorite vampire doll my parents gave me when I was a little girl. It's the one with the blond hair and the sharp jaw and the green eyes that almost look purple if you tilt his head under the light.

"Put that back."

Bonnie ignores me and pretends to make the vampire doll dance around my bed. "Spill the beans, Blair. Did you meet your future fangy husband last night?"

I sit up straighter. "I said, put it back."

Bonnie's brows shoot up. "What?"

"That doll. Put it back," I repeat, my voice clipped.

"Geez." She holds it higher, inspecting it like it's suddenly fascinating. "What crawled up your ass?"

"Nothing crawled up my ass."

"Sure." Bonnie snorts. "Because you're always *so* possessive over your creepy vampire doll."

"It's not creepy," I snap.

Bonnie's grin widens. "Oh my God. You're being so weird." I reach for it. She pulls it away.

"Bonnie," Mom says sharply. "Stop messing with your sister."

"Fine." Bonnie rolls her eyes and tosses the doll toward me, then flops back against my pillows. "Keep your creepy doll."

"Blair, honey, let's focus on the important things, shall we?" my mom requests as she sets her coffee down on my nightstand. This is her way of saying, *Don't even think about arguing with your sister right now.* "We need to make sure you're ready."

She's not wrong. The Selection and accompanying Bonding are coming up incredibly soon. The date won't be revealed until forty-eight hours prior, but once it's announced, I need to be ready to head to New York almost immediately.

"You want to go shopping with us, Bonbon?" my mom asks, and Bonnie groans.

"Do I have to?"

"It'd be nice to support your sister," my mom says, using guilt as her tactic of choice. "This is really important for her."

"Can't Blair just find a husband the good old-fashioned way?" Bonnie sighs. "I mean, it's all a little strange that she has to do these weird events to find a man. I don't get it. Are the men losers or something? Why can't they date like normal people?"

"Bonnie, when you're older, you'll understand why this is so important," Mom says. "And why it's actually a huge *privilege* that Blair gets to do this."

"Doubt it," Bonnie mutters. "And honestly, I'm just happy it's not me."

Happy it's not her? Obviously, my sister has no idea what she's talking about.

"But if it were you, Bonnie," Mom answers, despite the fact that she should just ignore her "then you wouldn't have a choice."

"Yeah, I would." Bonnie laughs. "I wouldn't go. No matter how much you tried to make me."

"You know what, Bonbon?" Mom sighs and pointedly uses her index finger to lift the skin on her forehead to prevent eleven lines. "I think now is the exact perfect time for you to get dressed and ready to go shopping with us. Otherwise, I'll end up needing an additional bottle of Botox at my next appointment."

"Speaking of creepy, Botox is, like, really bad for you, Mom. It's—"

"Bonnie!" Mom cuts her off and points toward my bedroom door. "Go get ready."

"Gawd." Bonnie flops off my bed dramatically. "This feels like oppression."

My mom ignores her this time and smiles over at me. "You think you can be ready in about an hour, Blair?"

I smile. "Definitely."

When they leave, the room goes quiet again, and I sit on the edge of my bed, picking the vampire doll back up and turning him around in my hands. The eyes catch the light and shift—green deepening into dark violet.

And instantly, my mind flashes back to last night.

To the man with the blond hair and green eyes who was watching me from across the room. I spent a lot of the night hoping he'd come and talk to me, but he never did.

Something uncomfortable rolls in my stomach, but I ignore it and shove out of bed, heading into the bathroom to turn on the shower.

But before I can hop in, my phone chimes on my nightstand with a text message.

> Holland Thorne: Morning, Blair. Hope you're
> feeling as incredible as you looked last night.
> Did you have a good time?

A smile tugs at my mouth before I can stop it. Holland Thorne is someone my parents have known for a few years. He's a vampire and holds an important position as a lawyer in the entertainment industry. He's only a few years older than me, and most of his clients are elites.

He's kind of a middleman for the elites, so to speak.

> Holland: Everyone loved you. And Damien? He
> couldn't stop talking about you.

I smile as I type quickly.

> Me: He talked about me?

I'm so tempted to ask more details about Damien, but I know that's not appropriate. That's not how these things are done. It's all very hush-hush.

> Holland: He noticed you, for sure. And, trust me,
> that's not something he does casually.

Damien is reserved—yes—but that just means when he chooses, it's significant. And if he spent most of last night talking to me and he even talked to Holland about me…that *has* to be a good thing.

Still, my fingers hover over the screen, and I find myself sending him another message.

> Me: Were there…others? Any other men asking
> about me?

The reply comes fast.

> Holland: Quite a few. You made an impression,
> Blair. So many men have you at the top of their
> list.

My heart does a silly little dance inside my ribs, and I glance down at the doll in my hand before I start typing another message.

> There was a man with green eyes and blond
> hair last night. He was wearing a black suit. Do
> you happen to know him?

But just before I can hit send, I delete the whole thing. It would be overstepping a serious line if I inquired about a specific elite vampire like that.

Don't be stupid, Blair, I tell myself, setting down my phone and forcing myself into motion instead.

Shower, makeup, hair, I get myself ready for the day.

By the time I come downstairs and walk out our front door, Bonnie is already sprawled across the back seat of the Bentley like a bored cat while Mom scrolls through emails on her phone beside her.

Our driver Loomis shuts my door with his usual quiet efficiency and pulls away from the house.

Bonnie makes my outfit the topic of discussion the second we pull onto the highway. "Wow. Nice dress," she says flatly. "You sure you don't want to save that outfit for the big sacrifice?"

Mom doesn't even look up from her phone. *"Bonnie."*

"What?" Bonnie shrugs, completely unrepentant. "That's what it is, right? A very glamorous sacrifice."

"If it were a sacrifice, that would involve death," I retort, rolling my eyes. "This involves marriage."

"And having a vampire's baby," Bonnie adds. "Sounds like a pretty big sacrifice to me."

Mom finally looks up then, giving Bonnie the same warning look she's been giving her since she turned into a teenage smartass.

Bonnie huffs out an annoyed sigh but sinks back into the leather seat. "Relax," she mutters. "I'm just saying I'm thrilled the vampire dating show isn't my problem."

An hour later, we're walking through the most expensive shopping district in Boston, the kind of fashion street where there are zero depressing-as-hell department stores and the sales associates greet my mother by name. Of course, Devney Windsor is in her element here. She moves through racks of designer labels like she's my actual stylist.

And my smartass little sister trails behind us, offering running commentary that no one asked for.

"That dress looks like a tablecloth."

"That one looks like a curtain."

"That one probably costs more than my future therapy bill."

"Bonnie." I shoot her a look. "You're supposed to be helping."

"I *am* helping," she says cheerfully. "I'm eliminating the bad options."

Somewhere between the third store and the fourth, a strange feeling starts to overcome me every time we walk out of a shop. It's just this faint pressure between my shoulder blades and reminds me of when someone's standing too close behind you.

I try to ignore it, but it doesn't go away.

If anything, it gets stronger.

I glance over my shoulder as we step out onto the sidewalk again, letting my gaze drift casually through the crowd.

But all I see are other shoppers, the occasional tourist, and businessmen with phones pressed to their ears, hurrying across the pavement.

Still… My pulse ticks up, and goose bumps pepper my arms and neck.

Bonnie bumps my arm as we walk. "You okay?"

"Fine," I lie, even though the feeling—an odd, prickling awareness—is still there.

I have no idea who or what or why it would be, though.

5

KANE

I'M NOT WHERE I'M SUPPOSED TO BE.

That's not a moral statement; it's a logistical one and, most likely, a big, *big* problem.

Calloway is in Concordia, ears open, doing what we agreed we'd do—watching for any sign the elites are looking for us and, most importantly, have clocked Worcester. That's where Rook and Kylie are still holed up in the hotel room. The last I heard from Rook was yesterday evening, and I think Kylie's at least willing to talk to him after we kidnapped her.

Prior to that, she'd locked herself in the bathroom and taken three showers.

It's a little complicated, to say the least. But then again, most relationships don't start with a kidnapping.

Cal and I have mostly stayed out of Rook's hair while he and Kylie figure shit out. We've focused on keeping our ears to the ground, hoping to devise some sort of preemptive move when the elites finally get around to hunting and killing us for our crimes.

Right now, I'm supposed to be with Cal in Concordia—our

hometown and the place we will most likely never be able to go back to after having taken Kylie Moon.

Instead, I'm just outside Boston, in a wealthy suburb, sitting across the street from a shopping district that looks like money built it just to prove it could. Pristine walking paths with perfect landscaping and storefronts that wouldn't dare advertise a sale. Only full price here, baby. Just luxury brands that expect you to drop five figures on a fucking pair of shoes.

Honestly, I wouldn't be surprised if the goddamn sidewalks are heated.

She steps out of one of the stores with two shopping bags in her hands and sunlight bouncing off her dark brown hair.

My chest tightens. And my eyes fixate.

Fuck me. Why is she so goddamn beautiful?

Her name is Blair Windsor, and as of last night, she's completely wrecked my fucking world without even saying a word to me.

Her mother, Devney Windsor, follows behind her, and her teenage sister, Bonnie Windsor, appears bored.

The knot in my stomach grows.

I definitely shouldn't be here. I should be in Concordia where Calloway is, keeping my ears open and making sure no one's sniffing too close to Worcester.

Instead, I'm watching a rich girl buy clothes with the sole purpose of "impressing her future vampire husband." A vampire husband who only exists in her mind, that is. The elites don't give a shit about wedding bells. They just want blood. And to breed.

My phone buzzes.

Cal: What are you doing right now?

I glance at the message and then at Blair across the street.

Me: Just a little surveillance.

It's not a lie. I mean, I am surveilling…*her.*

Blair laughs at something her little sister Bonnie says, nudging her gently with her elbow. Clearly, everything is peachy keen fucking jelly bean in her mind. She's going to find her prince charming vampire and live happily ever after once she's chosen by him at the Selection—or the "Choosing Ceremony," as she's eloquently dressed it up when talking about it with her mother.

Mind you, what Blair is excited about is not a choosing or a ceremony. It's a fucking auction where rich, vile bloodsuckers pay for her blood, for her virginity, and for the right to do as they please—for *her.* Like she's a damn Volkswagen.

There's nothing ceremonial or romantic about it.

Also, seeing as the first time I laid eyes on Blair Windsor was less than twenty-four hours ago and I know her full name and everyone in her family's names, I do realize I am well past stalker territory here.

Not to mention, the intense amount of eavesdropping I've been doing over the past two hours has given me a plethora of knowledge about Blair Windsor, and Google has certainly helped answer some of the questions I've had.

Blair Windsor is twenty-three years old.

Her father, Harry Windsor, is the CEO of a Fortune 500 company that sells medical devices, and he sits on several boards within the medical and tech communities. Her family isn't just rich, but *rich.* She's lived her entire life with a golden spoon in her pretty little mouth, and I couldn't be further from the type of man she's imagined in her mind.

I'm blue-collar, working class, and callused hands. To her, I'm probably no better than gum on the bottom of her shoe.

Unfortunately for me, I'm hopelessly locked in on her.

She's my fucking fate.

And it's really starting to make sense why Rook acted like a moron whenever Kylie was around.

Cal: Everything good?

I watch Blair flip her hair over her shoulder before pulling a tube of lip gloss out of her purse. Her younger sister Bonnie bounces around her, and Blair rolls her eyes while she slides the gloss over her luscious mouth.

My chest clenches, and a jolt zaps my fucking nerves at the sight of her perfect pink mouth.

And then my stupid phone buzzes in my pocket again.

Cal: Where are you?

Shit. I stare at it for a second too long.

Me: Concordia. Same as you.

I'm nowhere near Concordia right now, and this might be the first time I've ever lied to my brother about something this important.

Cal: Where at in Concordia?

Me: Just around. Trying to keep moving, you know? Not staying in one place for too long.

Cal: What are you seeing?

Fuck me. What is this, an interrogation?

I glance up. Blair laughs at something Bonnie says again. Devney doesn't laugh but gives a small smile, and I reckon that makes her a regular comedian. And they head to the next store.

> **Me:** Uh…nothing out of the ordinary. Nothing to worry about.

> **Cal:** Worcester was quiet when I was there. No tails on me coming or going. Kylie hasn't bolted.

> **Me:** How's Rook?

> **Cal:** He's good, actually.

> **Me:** So…it's working out?

> **Cal:** Well, fuck yeah, it's working out. Fated mates, bro.

Fated mates, bro. Yeah. Fucking tell me about it.

I look up from my phone on instinct, and Blair, her sister Bonnie, and her mom walk back out of a store and head to the next one. Must have been a disappointing showing in there.

> **Cal:** You seen Holland?

> **Me:** No.

> **Cal:** Well, if you see him, keep eyes on him. If he moves, I want to know.

I type back with my thumb without looking down, watching the sun bounce off Blair Windsor's hair and her pretty fucking skin instead.

> **Me:** You got it.

Across the street, Blair stops near a window display, adjusting her coat while Devney prattles on about some dress she thought Blair should've bought.

My phone buzzes for what feels like the millionth fucking time.

> Cal: Change of plans, let's meet up now.
> Describe the scene.

I hesitate. He wants to know where I am *right now*.
Shit.

> Me: Same old. Mall. Shops. People.

> Cal: Why are you at the fucking mall?

Across the street, Blair turns her head slightly, scanning the crowd before she refocuses on her mom as she talks intently about fashion choices and which stores they need to go to next.

> Cal: KANE

Just my name. All caps. No punctuation. That's Cal's version of a raised eyebrow.

> Me: So, funny story, I might not be in
> Concordia…

> Cal: Where the fuck are you?

I grimace as I type the truth.

> Me: Rich suburbs. Boston side.

> Cal: What in the fuck are you doing near
> Boston?

Because of her. *It's all because of her. Ever since last night, she's all I can think about. She's all I can sense. She's the only fucking thing on my goddamn mind.*

I don't answer right away because answering feels like admitting something I'm not ready to admit.

But then, something happens. For the first time in Holland Thorne's miserable fucking existence, he actually helps me. Across the street from where Blair stands on the sidewalk chatting with her mom and sister, Holland the slimefuck approaches from the valet stand. He looks like a douche in loafers and khakis and shiny Ray-Bans on his face.

He, of course, is showcasing that easy smile of his while his goons Mark and Evan flank him on either side.

At the sight of him, Blair and Devney smile, and even Bonnie offers a wave.

Clearly, the whole fucking Windsor family knows him.

That twist in my gut clenches tighter.

Holland kisses Devney's cheek like he belongs in her world. He speaks to Blair. She laughs and smiles like she hasn't a clue the true piece of shit that he is.

> **Cal: KANE WHAT THE FUCK ARE YOU DOING
> RIGHT NOW?**

It takes all my willpower to pull my attention away from Blair, but I manage to send Cal a quick message.

> **Me: Relax. I came here on a little bit of a whim,
> but it worked out. Slimefuck is here with his
> two goons.**

He knows who Slimefuck is instantly.

> **Cal: Keep eyes on him.**

Across the street, Holland leans in close to Blair, saying something low. Her expression shifts—excited, pleased, proud.

Devney nods, and a satisfied smile crests her mouth. Bonnie still looks bored. Frankly, I don't know the kid, but goddamn, she's growing on me. I'd be bored out of my mind if I had to stand there listening to Holland Thorne prattle on.

I open my ears and try to listen.

Something about *tomorrow.*

New York.

A penthouse.

Damien Snow.

Blair's heart is racing with excitement. And under all of that, even though Holland is a shield and I can't read his intention at all, his two brofers' intentions hum like a live wire. They have ulterior motives, and not a single one of them is being sincere right now.

But it's clear from their body language they want Blair to feel excited about the whole fucked-up situation they're planning for Damien Snow—a very important vampire elite.

I don't know Damien personally, but I know enough about him to know he's a vicious kind of man. He was the one at the preview last night smelling her fucking neck.

My jaw tightens, and I quickly shoot Cal a message back.

> **Me: He's currently setting up something for a woman who was at the preview.**
>
> **Cal: Anything about us?**
>
> **Me: We don't appear to be on his radar right now.**

Holland's only focused on Blair. He wants to sweet-talk her

as much as he can to make her willing and compliant. But she has no fucking idea how dark his mind probably is. How devious it all feels, just being able to read Mark's and Evan's intentions.

> **Cal: Don't do anything stupid. Let's head back
> to Worcester in about two hours.**

Don't do anything stupid? *It's starting to feel too fucking late for that.*

Across the street, Blair turns slightly. Her hair catches the light. She smiles at Holland like he's the bridge to everything she wants.

And inside my chest, the bond pulls so hard it feels like it's tearing something loose.

Tomorrow.

NYC.

Penthouse.

Damien Snow.

None of that sounds good.

If it's not the auction, it's against the rules to meet up for anything prior—and even her fairy-tale version of the Selection will be off the rails for good. If it is the auction, I'm out of time anyway. Plus, the mere idea of her going on a trip with anyone but me feels akin to murder.

Three birds, one stone, because really, I'm saving us both here.

Fuck. The narrative you're spinning sure as hell better hold up later, Kane.

Because there is no version of this where I walk away. And things are about to hit overdrive with absolutely no chance left for reverse.

6

Y SUITCASE SITS OPEN ON THE BENCH AT the foot of my bed, and I smooth my hands over a Hermes silk blouse before folding it carefully.

Normally, I would've had our housekeeper pack my bags—my mom had even insisted on that—but I don't know, this trip feels too special to leave it up to anyone else.

I *need* to make sure everything is perfect. *I need to make sure I don't let my mom down.*

I set the blouse gently atop a pair of jeans, but before I can grab the next shirt, my phone buzzes on my nightstand.

Holland: Tomorrow's confirmed. Car will pick you up at 7 a.m. sharp.

I smile, and my pulse flutters inside my chest. Tomorrow, I'm going to New York to spend the evening with *Damien Snow*, a vampire elite who's so interested in me he's made expensive arrangements to see me before the final choosing ceremony.

I found all this out this afternoon when Holland met up with my mom and Bonnie and me while we were shopping. And he waxed poetic about Damien's impressive penthouse in the middle of Manhattan. Apparently, it sits sixty stories up, and the view of Central Park is unreal.

I can only imagine what it looks like.

Looks like you're about to find out.

Another text chimes in.

> **Holland: Make sure you pack for a few days. Just in case.**

A few days? Last I heard, I was just flying out in the morning on Damien's private jet and I'd be back by the evening. Frankly, I didn't even know I could have a private meeting with one of the vampires before the Selection anyway, but with the way Holland explained it this morning, it's a very rare occurrence and reserved for only the best candidates.

I type back.

> **Me: A few days?**

> **Holland: It's a good thing, Blair. Damien really wants to get to know you. More than any of the other women from the event last night.**

He wants me more than all the other girls.

My cheeks warm at that, and my smile practically consumes my face. I can't help it. To have a man who's clearly so powerful, so important, want to get to know me feels unreal. It feels…amazing.

And Damien comes across as a reserved and careful kind of man. He's in total control. And men like that aren't impulsive. They choose carefully. They only want the best. *And he wants me.*

I glance down at the dress laid across my bed. It's this pale lavender silk that hugs my curves perfectly but isn't overtly obscene. It's sophisticated but discreetly sexy at the same time. My mom insisted I buy it today and bring it with me tomorrow.

I already had a cute black cocktail dress in mind, but since Holland is now saying a few days, I guess my new dress makes sense…

And if this is serious, if this is moving toward Damien choosing me, wouldn't it require more than one evening? It would be almost disrespectful to rush something so important.

My phone buzzes again.

> **Holland:** Also, I need to update you on some rules. Damien is a very discreet man. His privacy and your privacy are incredibly important to him, so there will be limited contact while you're there.

The warmth in my chest cools slightly, and my brow furrows at his words.

> **Me:** Limited contact? What does that mean?

> **Holland:** You'll need to leave your phone at your house. I'm sure you can understand that it's easier for both you and Damien if outside distractions are removed. Also, consider it a really good thing that he wants to be that focused on you. I don't know if I've ever seen him so…entranced. ;)

I swallow and glance toward the suitcase before moving my eyes back to the phone in my hands.

> **Me:** So, I can't bring my phone with me?

Holland: No, you cannot. But if you need to get in contact with anyone, Damien won't hesitate to oblige.

Ever since I got a phone in middle school, I can't remember a time I didn't have it with me. It seems very first-world problems, I know, but I can't deny my stomach pinches at the thought.

After Holland updated that Damien wanted to spend more time with me, my mom gushed. She'd never heard of private meet-ups like this before the Selection, but all that means is that it must be very rare and very exclusive. She was practically giddy over it all, to be honest.

Only important people know important things, Blair, she'd said. *And this means you're important.*

I just never imagined I'd be unreachable.

I try to picture it—being in a penthouse in Manhattan, city lights glittering below, Damien standing beside me—and not being able to text Bonnie or call my mom or dad.

It feels…off. Strange, even.

Don't be so freaking dramatic, I tell myself. *It's just because this is new. And new always feels a little unsettling at first.*

I walk to my vanity, staring at my reflection.

"This is your legacy," I whisper to my face in the mirror. "Your future. Your everything. This is the best thing that's ever happened in your life."

I open my phone again.

Me: Will my parents be able to check in?

The response is immediate this time.

Holland: Blair, you have nothing to worry about.
Trust me. Everything will be handled.

Trust me.

I exhale slowly.

Of course my parents wouldn't be cut off. That wouldn't make sense. This is prestigious. This is sophistication and royalty and wealth. It isn't some…disappearance.

It's a selection. A *choosing*. That's how we've always referred to it.

My parents trust these people. It's the inner circle they've been a part of my whole life. And it's just a couple of freaking days. It's not as if I'm being shipped off to Siberia, never to be heard from again.

My fingers hover over the screen. I almost send my mom a text message, asking her if she feels like it's okay, but I don't.

I'm an adult woman, for goodness' sake. This is my life. This is my future. I've totally got this.

I return to my suitcase and add another dress. Then heels. Then lingerie I bought months ago and pretended I wasn't buying for whatever vampire legend I ended up with.

Damien is a legend; Holland's made that clear.

And a few days is a good freaking thing. It's giving "he's serious about me" vibes.

I set my phone facedown on my nightstand, and I sit on the edge of my bed and try to summon the champagne feeling from this morning.

The floating. The certainty. It's there. *Mostly.*

On a whim, I grab my vampire doll from his spot on my shelf and tuck it into the side of my suitcase underneath some of my clothes. I know it's a little childish to bring a doll to a dalliance with a vampire, but he's always brought me comfort—and if I hide him well enough, no one has to know.

A soft knock taps against my door before it creaks open.

Bonnie slips inside without waiting for permission, wearing one of my oversized sweaters and fuzzy socks.

I almost startle, but with a wildly beating heart and every molecule of willpower, I stop myself. It'll only lead to questions I don't want to answer about my green-and-violet-eyed stowaway.

She leans against the doorframe and folds her arms. "So," she says.

"So…?" I ask.

"You're really going tomorrow."

I roll my eyes. "Bonnie. Not this again." Ever since she heard about my trip tomorrow, she's been telling me not to go.

"No, I mean it." She pushes off the door and wanders farther into the room. "You're flying to New York to spend the day with some mysterious man named Damien, and everyone's acting like it's the most romantic thing that's ever happened."

"Well…it kind of is."

She walks over to my bed and looks inside my suitcase. "Doesn't this feel weird to you?"

"No."

"Not even a little?"

"It feels exciting, Bon."

She makes a face. "It feels like a very classy version of an ar-ranged marriage."

"It's not arranged."

"Blair," she says dryly, "you've been raised your whole life knowing some vampire was eventually going to pick you. You're a twenty-three-year-old virgin because you're literally saving yourself for the big *bonding night* that Mom's talked about for years."

"What does my virginity have to do with anything?" I question, but then my eyes go wide when realization hits me. "Bonnie, you are only fifteen years old. I swear on everything, if you let that prick boyfriend of yours take your virginity, I will murder him."

"Relax." She snorts. "I wouldn't let someone named Josh get my V-card. I'm saving myself for Harry Styles, and anyway, this conversation isn't about me, Blair. It's about you and your soon-to-be arranged marriage. Which is weird. Like, really weird."

"It's tradition, Bon." I laugh despite myself.

"*Tradition*," she mocks immediately. "The generational skips are the best thing that's ever happened to my future. I don't want to be married off to Count Dracula."

I shake my head and fold another shirt. "You say that now."

"No," she says. "I mean it. You get the fancy vampire husband and the mysterious elite life. I get to marry a normal human who eats pizza and doesn't drink my blood."

"Dang, sis. Dramatic much?"

Her sarcasm fades a little as she watches me toss another shirt into my suitcase. "You're not nervous?"

"A little," I admit. "But that's normal."

"I guess." She shrugs, but the edge of concern lingers in her voice. "I just don't love the idea of you flying off to meet some man none of us actually knows."

"He's part of the inner circle," I remind her.

"That's the part that makes it weird."

I walk over and bump my shoulder into hers. "I'll be fine. I promise."

"You better be."

"I will."

"Well, I guess I'll let you get back to packing, then." She turns to leave but hesitates in my doorway. "Blair?"

"Yeah?"

"If he turns out to be creepy, just text me and I'll come to New York and drag you home myself."

I grin. "Thanks, Bon, but I'm certain everything is going to be good."

"Whatever you say." She rolls her eyes at my confidence but smiles a little before disappearing down the hall.

Once I finish packing my suitcase and get ready for bed, I lie back against my pillows and stare at the ceiling.

Tomorrow, I will be one step closer to being chosen.

And that's a privilege…*right?*

Right. Yes. *Of course,* it's a freaking privilege.

I've been waiting my *whole* life for this.

7

KANE

THE SKY IS STILL SLATE GRAY. THERE ARE NO BIRDS chirping yet and no cars moving about on the road. Just morning frost clinging to hedges and a house too large to feel real in this light.

My phone buzzes in the cupholder as I idle at the end of a private drive lined with iron gates and trimmed hedges. The Windsor family mansion gives main character energy as it dominates the landscape. Beautiful stone, black shutters, and security cameras tucked under eaves, it's the kind of house that assumes nothing bad ever happens here.

Even though something bad is happening right fucking now.

I steal a glance at the screen of my phone.

> **Cal: ETA?**

I should answer. I don't.

But my phone buzzes again.

> **Cal: You good?**

Well, shit. I type fast, coming up with a lie as quickly as I can.

> **Me: Just checking one more thing. Headed your
> way after.**

I toss my phone back into the cupholder and move my gaze right back to the house.

She's inside it; I can feel her. But that's probably because the bond isn't subtle when I'm this close to her. If anything, it's downright choking with how much it's pulling me from the inside out.

She's awake. She's excited. Her body hums with nervous anticipation. Blair Windsor thinks all her dreams are about to come true.

Beneath her naïveté, I feel layers of cold and indifference. Five miles out, my body senses a black SUV with two gofer elites inside. And I can feel their intent like smoke in my fucking lungs.

They're here to collect. And while Blair thinks she's coming back home to her parents' mansion after a few days, these fucking gofers know the truth—she might not come back at all.

Cal's last text sits unanswered on the screen.

> **Cal: Make it quick. The sooner we're all there,
> the better.**

He's talking about the cabin in the woods. The one Rook, Cal, and I built with our own bare hands. The one that's off-the-grid and hidden beneath forest so dense no one ever dares to explore.

Cal is on his way there.

Rook is there with Kylie now.

And I *should* be there too.

Instead, I'm here, watching Blair walk out the front door of her parents' mansion with a fancy white suitcase that probably costs more than the Suburban I'm sitting in.

She turns back toward the front door and fiddles with something, and then the iron gates open at the end of the driveway.

She's dressed to the nines in a sophisticated outfit of sleek black pants, a black blazer with a small white top underneath, and black heels with shiny red bottoms. She looks stunning, unequivocally beautiful, and my chest aches over the fact that she thinks she's heading toward somewhere good.

Yesterday, after eavesdropping on her conversation with Holland while she was shopping with her mother, I found out Damien Snow wants her to spend time with him at his fancy penthouse in New York.

Her mother approved because her intentions make it clear she doesn't know any better. Her human fragility has made it impossible for her to see past the curtain, to the evil vampire wizards who plan to destroy her daughter in ways far beyond her comprehension.

I shake my head. Refusing to let my mind go there. Refusing to think about the true realities of her situation.

But fuck me. I can't just stand here and watch her get into a car with gofers and drive away.

I put the engine in drive and head down the driveway, through the now-open gates.

Fuck. What am I doing?

I keep driving.

This is a bad idea. This is such a bad fucking idea.

I keep driving.

Blair glances down the long expanse of her parents' driveway, and when her eyes catch sight of my Suburban pulling in, I can feel her blood pump harder. Feel her pulse start to pick up with excitement.

Turn around. Turn the fuck around and leave.

She waves her hand toward me, and I keep driving, not coming to a stop until I'm about twenty feet away from her.

You are so fucking fucked right now. So fucking fucked!

I don't know what I'm doing, but I step out of the driver's seat. And the instant our eyes meet, I feel like my heart is trying to claw its way out of my chest.

Her breath hitches, and her brows lift in immediate recognition. "Do I know you?"

"Not exactly." *But I certainly know you. Because you're mine.*

She digs her teeth into her bottom lip. "Wait… I think you were at… I think I saw you the other night. At an event."

I shake my head. "Probably not."

Her eyes search mine intently. "No, I'm pretty sure you were there." And she continues to study me openly—her gaze taking in my blond hair and green eyes. "I'm almost positive you were there. Though, you never came over to talk to me."

So, she noticed me too?

Get it together, you fucking idiot. Now isn't the time for lovey-dovey bullshit when there's a car full of gofers on their way.

"Maybe you're confusing me with someone else."

"Oh, okay…" She pauses and glances down at her suitcase. "But you're the one picking me up?"

The lie is right there. I mean, I could just tell her *yes, I'm picking you up. Hop in!* and rescue her from this fucked-up situation she doesn't even realize is happening.

But lying to her feels akin to burning myself alive. It's stupid.

And I wish I weren't ruled by a reckless captain right now, but I am. Every bit of the bond is in control.

"You can't go."

Her head jerks back. "What?"

"It's not what you think it is."

"Excuse me?" she questions and takes a pointed step away from me.

All the while, I can feel the SUV and the men who are prepared to take her getting closer.

"Blair, don't go with them."

"H-how do you know my name?" Her breath picks up speed. "What are you doing here? Who are you?"

Fuck. I can smell her fear of me. Feel the terror in her fucking veins. And the irony is that I'm not the one she should be scared of.

"You need to leave," she says. "Right now."

"You're in danger."

"Danger?" She stares at me like I've lost my mind. "From whom?"

"You need to go back inside the house. Don't go with them."

"You sound insane." Her voice is rising, and I start to fear she's going to draw attention to the men who are on their way or to her family that's still sleeping or to whatever security cameras might be facing our direction. "You need to leave. Right now."

The men are getting closer. And I can feel the shift in the air as they take the final turn toward this neighborhood.

"You don't understand what they are," I say.

"You are a crazy person. Leave right now."

"You aren't being chosen for marriage," I say, forcing the words out clean. "They just want to use you. Destroy you."

Her spine goes rigid. Her eyes wide.

But the sound of an engine reaches the edge of my hearing, and I know the gofers are hardly a minute away.

"If you go with them," I say, "you won't come back the same. You might not come back at all."

"I'm going inside," she says in a rush. "I'm calling the police." She starts to turn for her parents' big fucking mansion, but the engine hum reaches the driveway before Blair reaches the door.

A black Escalade with tinted windows rolls through the open iron gates and slows near the front steps.

"Thank God." Blair exhales, relief flooding her features. "They're here."

Two men step out, and I know them immediately.

Mark and Evan—Holland's buddies and hockey teammates from the league my brothers and I play in at Concordia Rec Rink. Well, hockey league we *used* to play in. There's not much hockey-playing happening at the moment. We're apparently a little busy saving women from the fucking elite and trying not to get killed in the process.

They don't recognize me at first, but that's because they're focused on Blair and getting her where their masters want her to go.

But when their eyes shift past her and land on me, everything changes.

"What the fuck?" Evan mutters.

"Fucking Kane Slater?" Mark breathes.

"Surprise, motherfuckers," I say. I'm smiling on the outside. Though, on the inside, I'm definitely on edge. Two against one isn't easy. Not impossible—*I'll fucking kill them if they try to touch her*—but not easy.

"You've got to be kidding me." Evan lets out a short, humorless laugh. "You got a death wish or something, Slater?"

"Wait…" Blair looks between us. "You know him?"

Mark's mouth curves slowly. "Oh, we know him."

Evan shakes his head once. "Every elite in the area is looking for you and your idiot fucking brothers."

"You're bold showing up here," Mark adds. "Thought you three were hiding."

"Thought you'd be smarter than this," Evan says, eyes narrowing. "After what your brother pulled."

Kylie. They mean Kylie.

"By the way, not only do the elites want you three dead, they want her dead too," Mark says casually, like he's discussing the weather. "Whole mess goes away that way."

"What are you talking about?" Blair goes rigid beside me. "Want who dead?"

"It's nothing for you to worry your pretty little head about," Mark reassures, a slimy smile intact on his lips. "But let me guess, sweetheart, this man here was bothering you, huh?"

Blair looks at me again, her eyes searching my face and her mind trying to understand who to believe. But when Evan takes it upon himself to step toward her, I can't hold myself back.

"Don't fucking touch her," I say.

Mark laughs. "You know, this probably is for the best, Ev. We can solve two problems at the same time."

Evan grins. "Good point."

Their intent shifts instantly. No longer focused on escorting Blair, they are one hundred percent focused on me.

On *killing* me.

Evan moves first. He's fast—vampire-fast like the rest of us—and I don't miss the flash of a blade from inside his jacket.

He goes for my throat, and I pivot and catch his wrist mid-strike, twisting hard enough that the blade drops to the ground.

It doesn't stop him, though. He drives forward, pushing his full body weight toward me like a fucking linebacker, but I adjust my hips and use his momentum to slam his body into the stone column beside the front steps of the Windsors' mansion.

The impact is heavy but muted.

He recovers quickly, getting to his feet swinging, but I'm too fast for him. It's as if I can read his intentions before his brain can fully process them. In under a second, I'm behind him, his neck is in my hands, and I snap the life out of him.

I catch him before he hits the ground and lower him silently into the frost-covered grass of the Windsors' yard.

Blair screams at the sight of it.

Fuck. I'm sorry, Blair. I'm so sorry. I almost tell her exactly that—*want to tell her*—but Mark snarls as he heads straight for me.

He's older and stronger, and his eyes flash red as he lunges for me. He manages to tackle me away from the steps and the house.

Smart move, I'll give him that.

We crash into a manicured hedge, and he drives his forearm into my throat so hard I cough from the impact.

"You should've stayed hidden," he growls.

"And miss out on the chance to kill you?" I answer, my voice strangled. "Hell no."

He reaches for the gun in his holster, but I don't give him a chance. I hook his arm, reverse leverage, and slam him hard into the ground.

His head cracks against the stone edging.

He tries to recover, but I don't let him. I grab his jaw and twist with all my strength.

At first, there's resistance. But then, there isn't.

The snapping sound is brief, contained, and I hold him there a second longer before I let him fall with a thud into the yard.

Silence settles back over the driveway. No alarms. No lights flicking on.

Just frost, exhaust smoke, and two dead gofers on Windsor property.

Blair is staring at me like the world just split open.

"You killed them," she whispers, her hand going to her mouth. "They were supposed to take me to the airport! They were here to be my escorts, and you killed them!"

"You have no idea what these men had in store for you, Blair," I say, slowly walking toward her with both of my hands held in the air. "They don't give a fuck about you. Not them. Not Damien. Not any of the elites you know."

"Oh my God!" Her face drains of color. "You're insane!"

"You need to come with me, Blair."

"Help! Someone, help me!" Her scream cuts through the morning air, and I just…act.

As quick as I can, I pull her toward me, toss her over my shoulder, and walk straight past Mark and Evan's lifeless bodies lying in her parents' yard, heading straight for the Suburban. Blair thrashes against me, silent panic flooding her system.

She's kicking and screaming the entire way, her intentions clearly indicating that I'm ruining her big chance of being chosen. That I'm ruining her future. That I'm the villain.

Fuck. If you only knew what I'm saving you from. If you only knew, you wouldn't be screaming.

Instantly, the screaming stops.

I don't know why. I don't care why. Because all I can do right now is toss her in the back seat of the Suburban. She's fighting me the entire time, but her human strength and speed are nothing compared to mine.

I fucking hate that I have to restrain her with rope I snagged from the trunk to keep her secured in the back seat. Hate that I'm having to do any of this right now. Hate myself a million times over. But I'm doing it all anyway.

Because I don't have a choice.

Because I can't let anything happen to her.

Because I *have* to protect her.

Because Blair Windsor is mine, even if she doesn't know it yet.

8

BLAIR

*O*H MY GOD, I'VE BEEN KIDNAPPED!

My wrists are restrained—not painfully, but firmly—with something soft, and no matter how much I thrash around in the back seat, I can't get loose.

"You have lost your mind!" I scream. "Let me go! Let me fucking go!"

But he doesn't flinch. He just keeps driving.

Long fingers, strong wrists, and thick, corded veins visible beneath the skin, his hands are steady on the wheel. Those hands just picked me up as if I weighed nothing. They look like they can crush on demand. *Those hands just killed two men!*

"Ahhh!" I scream at the top of my lungs. "Oh my God! Stop the car! Let me out! I don't want to die! I'm too young to die!"

The world is moving too fast.

Trees blur past the windows in streaks of brown and green. The sky is bleeding from gray to pale pink, and I am in the back seat of an SUV with a man who just kidnapped me—and killed two freaking people and will probably kill me next!

"Ahhhhhh!" I scream again. And again. And again. And I don't stop screaming until my sobs roll one into another.

"*Blair*," he says. "It's okay. I promise. You're safe. I'm not going to hurt you. I'd **never** fucking hurt you."

"**Do not say my** name like you know me!" I shout at the top of my lungs, tears flowing down my cheeks. "You don't know me!"

"**I do know you**," he says. "I fucking know you more than I know myself."

"**What does that** even mean?" I shout. "Who are you? Why are you doing this to me?"

"**Because I have** to protect you."

"**Protect me?**" I cry. "You kidnapped me!" I lean as far forward as the restraints allow. "You took me against my will!"

"**I rescued you** before they could take you."

"**What are you** even talking about?!"

"**I'm talking about** fucking Holland. I'm talking about the fucking elites. I'm talking about Damien. I'm talking about what I just saved you from."

My body stills, and I stare at him in the rearview mirror. His green eyes are just as recognizable as I thought they were when he first showed up in my driveway. "It *is* you! You were at the preview, weren't you?" I yell at him. "You were there! I remember you!"

He doesn't say anything.

"**Why are you doing** this?" I cry. "You didn't even talk to me the other night, but now, you're kidnapping me? This doesn't make any sense. Is this some kind of game? Some kind of ego thing? A competition with Damien?"

"**This has nothing** to do with ego, Blair."

"**Stop saying my** name like you know me!"

He doesn't say anything after that. Instead, he keeps his eyes on the road, and I fight against the restraints in the back seat, trying everything I can to get out of them. My lungs scream out for help the entire time.

But when I look up, my eyes don't miss the way light hits his face. The way his blond hair shimmers or the way his green eyes turn almost violet.

And I freeze.

Because I *know* that face.

The hair.

The jaw.

The eyes.

The blond vampire doll with the green-violet eyes that I love so much—live and in person.

I shove the thought away instantly, mentally chastising myself. *Oh my God, Blair, this is clearly not that! This is a freaking kidnapping by a deranged psycho! He will probably murder you!*

"W-why are you doing this?" I ask him again.

"Because those men aren't who you think they are. Because they plan to destroy you."

"Oh my God!" I shout out in frustration. "You think my family would send me somewhere unsafe? Are you for real right now?"

Silence.

"You think my mom doesn't know what she's doing?" I scream. "You really think she would put me in harm's way?"

Still, silence.

He doesn't look at me. And somehow, that makes it worse.

I stare at the side of his face instead, at the straight line of his nose and the tight set of his mouth. He doesn't look wild. He doesn't look unhinged. He looks completely in control, which is very confusing for someone who just got kidnapped by him.

"You think it's a fairy tale," he says, his voice low in a way that urges goose bumps to roll up my arms. "But it's not."

"You don't know anything about what I think or don't think."

"I do." His voice is so certain that it makes me angry.

"No, you do not! You don't know anything about me!"

I look out the window, and a pit forms in my stomach as the road narrows and the trees grow denser and all signs of civilization begin to fade into forest.

"Where are we going?" I demand. "Where are you taking me?"

"Somewhere safe."

"Somewhere safe? Somewhere safe?! I was at my house! I was safe until you freaking kidnapped me!"

He glances at me over his shoulder, and something in his eyes makes my stomach drop. "You weren't safe," he says. "You weren't safe at all."

I hate that my pulse stutters at the way he says it, like he knows something I don't. Because there is no freaking way he knows anything about me or what the future holds for me. He clearly has no clue that he's quite possibly ruined my entire life.

"You're wrecking everything," I whisper, tears burning unexpectedly behind my eyes. "You have no idea what you've done. What you're keeping me away from."

He looks forward again. "I know exactly what I'm keeping you away from."

The quiet conviction in his voice is more terrifying than if he'd yelled.

I look away from him, but I can't stop seeing it.

Blond hair.

Green eyes.

The doll.

The way, for one horrible second, when he looked at me—it didn't feel like I was being taken. It felt like I was being protected. And more than that, like I was being *claimed.*

I don't know which one scares me more—so I settle for being freaked the fuck out enough for both.

9

KANE

ITH BLAIR SLUNG OVER MY SHOULDER, I push open the front door to the cabin. Arms flailing, heels kicking, body twisting with all her strength, she's fighting like hell as I step inside and kick the door shut with my boot.

"What the fuck?" Rook questions, his eyes darting between me and the woman slung over my shoulder.

"Holy shit, Kane!" Cal shouts, already on his feet.

"She's fine," I say, breathless but controlled. "I mean, she's real fucking pissed at me, but she's fine. She's safe."

That part matters the most to me. She's safe, even if she hates me for it.

Kylie's eyes go wide, and Rook moves instantly, pulling her into his side. He's protective, as he should be. Not only do the elites want us dead, but they also want anyone associated with us dead too. And well, he doesn't know the full reality of this just yet, but I've made shit a hell of a lot worse with what I've just done.

Blair bucks harder, and I adjust my grip on her waist.

"Who is she?" Cal asks.

"Her name is Blair."

The second Rook's eyes lock on hers, something shifts. He goes still, and it's then that I register she's still thrashing but she's not screaming. I can feel her lungs working, but she's not making any noise at all.

I frown slightly. *Is that because of me?*

Rook meets my eyes. His brow is furrowed, and his mouth is set in a firm line. It's clear not only is my elder brother reading Blair's thoughts right now, but he would appreciate an explanation for my current situation. "Kane, why do you have her?"

"I had to," I say. "I had to save her."

I feel Blair's chest move with force against my back, and I know she's trying to scream. But again, nothing comes out.

Rook's astute gaze flicks from her to me and back to her.

And that's when I feel it—*the bond.* Even with her this pissed at me, even with her thinking I'm some kind of lunatic who has ruined her life, the draw to her is pulsing inside my ribs. I can feel her intentions bleeding into my veins, into my mind, and I know without a doubt she's still too fucking naïve for her own well-being.

I know that her screams are being directed at the wrong people.

And I know that I'm able to stop them.

Holy fuck.

I swallow and focus on trying to explain. "She thought she was being chosen," I expand. "Thought it was an honor. A fucking privilege. She was just going to walk into the viper's fucking den willingly. She has no idea what they were planning to do to her."

That part makes my jaw tighten.

Because she really didn't know. Still doesn't know. She

thought Damien Snow was a potential fairy-tale fucking husband. Thought it was exciting to get to fly to New York and spend time at his penthouse. Thought it was just the beginning of this new, glamorous life she's been preparing for since she was a kid.

"Fuck me," Cal sighs. "You met her at the preview, didn't you?"

"What preview?" Rook asks, his head swiveling back and forth between the two of us.

But neither one of us wants to admit to him the big risk we took by following Holland to that masquerade party—the same event that Holland planned on bringing Kylie to.

Cal's jaw ticks as he stares at me. "I can't believe you kept this from me."

He's pissed. And I don't blame him. I've kept him completely in the dark on purpose like a total fucking asshole.

"She didn't know the truth, Cal!" I snap. "She thinks it's some kind of fucking fairy tale! Her goddamn mother was helping her shop for clothes! I couldn't not step in. I couldn't not save her. I had to. I fucking had to."

I don't mention Mark. Or Evan. Or the fact that I left their lifeless bodies in front of the Windsor mansion. I also make a concerted effort not to think about it, so Rook can't use his telepathy voodoo on my brain. It's an unfair omission, but fuck, my brothers aren't ready to hear the rest of this story. They're not ready to learn that I've probably—definitely—put us in an all-out war with the elites.

"Fuck, Kane," Rook mutters. "Fucking fuck."

"She thinks she knows," I continue. "But she has no clue. I

couldn't let her go there. I had to stop it." Because if I hadn't, the odds of her coming back were zero.

"You're locked in," Rook whispers.

Cal's head snaps toward him.

"This isn't just any woman, Cal," Rook says. "This is *her*."

The word lands heavier than it should.

Her.

Fated mate.

Mine.

"Oh fuck," Cal breathes. "Oh fuck, fuck, fuck, Kane. Do not tell me this is what I think it is. Please, do not fucking tell me."

Sorry, brother, but it is. It most certainly is.

I adjust a still-bucking Blair on my shoulder. And I know it's high time I stop tiptoeing around the truth. Clearly, my brothers know.

"Cal, you remember when you asked Rook if it was immediate with Kylie?" I toss out, my voice sounding steadier than I feel. Between the pulsing bond that threads me to Blair and the reality of what I've done, I'm a bundle of nerves. "Well, I can confirm that it is, in fact, immediate."

Rook looks up toward the ceiling, running a hand through his dark hair.

Cal stares at me with his jaw gaped open.

Both of their minds are probably racing with the reality—I'm still twenty-seven years old. The change, *this bond*, isn't supposed to be possible until I turn twenty-eight. And sometimes, even then, it can take male vampires until they're thirty to find their fated mate.

As far as we all know, this is too early. This shouldn't even be possible. And yet my body recognized her like it had been waiting for her for centuries.

Silence crashes down around us.

Blair is still fighting me. She's still terrified and thinking I ruined her life. And she most certainly has no clue that I just declared open war to keep her breathing.

The elites won't call this a misunderstanding. They'll call it retaliation. Add in the fact that they were already hunting us because of Kylie, and it's clear shit has hit the proverbial fan.

Not only did I kill two more of their gofers, I took from an important elite. Damien Snow believes Blair is his, and I've stopped that. To him, to them, I've stolen something they believe is rightfully theirs.

They won't ignore that. They won't forgive it.

And the irony of it all? Blair Windsor doesn't even want to be here.

But I'd rather she hate me than be dead.

If I could do it all over again, I'd do worse if I needed to. For her.

That realization settles deep in my chest like a promise.

This war isn't theoretical anymore.

It's here.

And I just lit the match.

10

H IS NAME IS KANE.

And though he might look similar, he is *nothing* like the fantasy man represented by my doll.

He's domineering and preachy, and every time I question the insane choice to kidnap me, he plays it off like he's some kind of savior.

As if his behavior isn't bad enough, he's not alone in this charade either. I don't know how many other people are here, but I know no one told Kane he was acting like an insane person. No one tried to assist me. No one tried to remove me from his shoulder and help me escape.

Which makes them, at the very least, complicit.

Now, he's carrying me up a flight of stairs like I weigh nothing, like I may as well be a freaking jacket made out of feathers. He moves down a hallway, the heavy sounds of his boots echoing inside my ear with each step, and he doesn't stop walking until we're in a small, depressingly rustic room.

When my eyes catch sight of a bed, fear clutches my throat.

He drops me onto it, and my body hits the mattress with a gentle thud.

Instantly, I scramble upright and put as much distance between him and me as I can, my body shaking at thoughts of the worst. I've already lost my autonomy; I can't lose my virginity too. Not like this.

"Why are you doing this?" I scream, the sound tearing out of my throat so hard it aches. "What do you want from me?" My voice is so loud and so real that it bounces off the walls.

For a split second, I sit there in shock. Earlier, in my driveway, and when we came into the house, I was trying to yell so hard that my throat burned, but there was no sound. And now it's back.

He turns calmly, shuts the door, and I don't miss how the metallic lock clicks deliberately into place. I'm overwhelmed and terrified, and I know without a doubt that I have nothing to lose. It never gets better from this point on when I watch crime shows—it gets messy and violent.

"You cannot lock me in here!" I shout, jumping off the bed and storming toward him. "Do you know who I am? Do you understand the mistake you've made?"

"Yes, I know who you are." The calm in his voice makes me want to throw something. "But this wasn't a mistake. This was necessary, Blair. For both of us."

"I was supposed to be in New York!" I yell. "I was supposed to be meeting someone very important. I was supposed to—"

"I know what you think you were supposed to be doing," he cuts me off. "But it's bullshit. It's not the truth at all."

"You don't know anything!" I scream, moving toward the door with the confidence of a woman free to walk through it, but he blocks me off completely by putting his big, intimidating body in my way.

I shift on my feet and head toward the window. I try to pull it up, and when it doesn't budge, I look for a latch or a switch, but there's none to be found. Still, I yank harder on it, as if maybe I can just tear the damn thing from the wall.

But when nothing happens, I turn to face him again. He's infuriatingly calm, like he didn't just kidnap me after committing murder.

"You are insane!" I spit, turning back toward him. "This is psychotic! *You* are psychotic! You can't just keep me here against my will!"

He doesn't argue; he doesn't need to. I'm locked in, and even if I weren't, he's bigger and faster and stronger. I don't stand a chance, and he knows it. Instead, he turns toward the closet and pulls out a fresh shirt. He tosses it on the bed and starts unbuttoning his flannel, and a new level of panic sets in. Not only is he keeping me here, but he also seems to be keeping himself here too.

With him actively undressing, my earlier worst-case scenario comes into sharper focus.

"Excuse me?" I blink what feels like a thousand times, trying to sound more outraged than scared. "What are you doing?"

"Changing my shirt." As he peels it off, I finally notice the dark stains across the fabric.

I don't know if it's blood or mud from my parents' yard, but either way, the reason he's covered in it is the same—he killed two freaking men in my driveway.

He tosses the shirt into the hamper and reaches for the clean one on the bed.

My eyes move from his face to his bare chest, and I instantly regret it. Thick but lean muscles sit beneath tanned skin, and every movement he makes showcases a flex of strength and power. It's no wonder he was able to kill people. It's no wonder he was able to carry me around like a sack of potatoes. It's no freaking wonder.

But my stupid eyes keep looking at him, taking in the way his biceps curl as he pulls his shirt over his head and catching the final sight of the thick V muscle that starts at his hips and disappears beneath his jeans.

Heat blooms low in my stomach before I can stop it.

No, Blair. Absolutely not. He is a murderer! A freaking kidnapper!

"You're an insane person," I snap, because anger is safer than acknowledging what just happened inside me. "You realize that, right? Everything you've done today is a serious crime!"

"I'm not insane," he says, and it's downright confusing how calm and controlled he appears. "But I can understand why you'd think that right now. You've been lied to and robbed of half the story, and everything about the way we've had to start this relationship lowers your trust."

This *relationship?* He must be joking. I don't need him understanding me. I don't need him to earn my trust. I need him to *let me go.*

If I can make it back to my parents' house soon, I can call Holland and find another way to get to New York, where Damien Snow is waiting for me. The chances were high that he could've chosen me as his mate and set me up for life.

And instead, I'm here. In this filthy, simple cabin with an insane but handsome man.

A man who's ruined *everything.*

My feet are moving before my brain can catch up with what I'm doing. Between one blink and the next, I'm standing right in front of him, and then, I slap him straight across the face as hard as I can.

The crack echoes off the walls of the small bedroom, but he doesn't move. He doesn't flinch. He doesn't even blink.

And my palm burns like I just attempted to hit a freaking statue.

"I hate you!" I push against his chest with both hands. "You've ruined my life!" I shove him again and again and again, but nothing happens. He doesn't shift his balance, doesn't take a step back. He just stands there, both feet steady on the ground, gaze squarely on me.

His eyes are an incredible shade of green, but for the briefest second, they showcase a violet undertone.

Déjà vu hits me like a truck, and a vision of my childhood doll fills my head again. My breath catches, but I force the bubbling thoughts out of my head.

But that memory isn't the only one that wants to come to the surface out of the now open hatch. Visuals of the men in my driveway and how fast they went from standing to lifeless on the ground. Him standing over them without so much as a labored breath. His eyes cutting to me.

It all happened so fast. Too fast. I didn't see his hands move. I didn't see him strike.

"You…" My voice wavers. "You moved so fast in my driveway. And…and…and you killed them. You killed those two men."

"Yes." The word is steady. No apology. No hesitation. No denial.

"And earlier…" I swallow hard against the tightness in my throat. "I was screaming…" I pause, but he says nothing. "I remember screaming." I keep going. "But I couldn't hear myself. Nothing was coming out of my mouth."

He stares at me patiently as pieces of comprehension begin to click into place. Human men don't hold power like that—only vampires do. They have powers beyond human understanding or capabilities.

"You're a vampire," I whisper. "I know you're a vampire, but you're not…" I swallow. "You live in a cabin. In the woods."

"Yeah," he says, qualifying, "Well, for now, at least."

"You're not rich?"

"No." He shakes his head. "I'm a repo man."

"You're a what?"

"A repo man. I repossess shit for a living. Cars. Trucks. Furniture, jewelry, whatever people don't pay on. It's my job to take it back."

"You work a blue-collar job?"

He nods.

"But h-how can you be a vampire if you're blue-collar?" That word unsettles me more than the killing. My whole life, I've been told *all* vampires are elite. All vampires are rich and powerful men.

If he's not elite, then that means that I've been lied to… My mother would never.

"No, clearly, that can't be true," I try to refute. "Clearly, you're not telling me the truth."

"I would never lie to you, Blair."

It's such a strange thing, standing in front of this man, and knowing I should feel frightened. I should be trying to claw my way out of this stupid cabin. But it's as if every cell in my body knows he's not going to kill me or do something terrible to me.

Which is crazy. I should be downright terrified. All the evidence supports a gruesome finish to this spectacularly messed-up day, not something sexy.

My pulse is racing now, neediness overcoming fear in the most infuriating way. Standing this close to him feels like I'm standing near live electricity. My skin feels too tight. My lungs feel too small. And my body wants to move closer to him.

"What's your name, then?" I question. "If you would never lie to me, what's your name?"

"Kane Slater."

I guess I thought he'd given me a fake name or something. I don't know what I expected his answer to be, but it wasn't that.

"You were at the mixer the other night, weren't you?" I demand. "I remember making eye contact with you."

"Yes." He nods. "I was there, but I wasn't there for the same reasons that men like Damien or Holland were there."

"Why were you there, then?"

"To get information," he says. "And to find you."

"Find me?" I narrow my eyes. "W-what?"

"Destiny, Blair," he says. "You are my destiny." My heart skips a beat and my head swims. And for some insane reason, I find myself taking a step toward him. And then another step. And then another.

Oh my God, what am I doing? Stop.

"You kidnapped me," I say, keeping my feet planted firmly to the ground. I need to anchor myself to something. I need to remind myself of what he just did.

"Yes, but not because I want to hurt you. Because I want to protect you."

"But you ruined my life."

"No, Blair." Even though my feet are still planted, he steps closer. "I *saved* your life."

My back bumps against the wall, but I don't remember him moving. Our chests are pressed against each other, and his eyes are locked on mine.

So close. So warm. So solid.

I should be scared.

You are scared, I tell myself. *He killed two men without blinking. He controlled my voice. He locked me in a room. This is scary. He is scary.*

And yet, my body leans toward him.

He closes his hand around my wrist, and my pulse jumps violently under his thumb. He raises my hand above my head and presses his body tighter against mine. Or maybe I'm pressing my body tighter against his. I don't know.

"All I want to do is protect you," he whispers back. "That's it. I simply *have to* protect you."

Heat spreads through my body from the contact, and goose bumps roll up my arms. It's as if my body is revolting against me. It's as if my body just wants to get as close to him as it can. It's confusing. It's overwhelming. It's consuming.

"I hate you," I say, but it sounds diluted now thanks to the rapid breaths of a wanton woman I can't seem to control.

His eyes turn violet. "Do you?"

I don't answer. I can't answer. My body is betraying me, and all I can think about is the way his mouth would feel against mine.

This man kidnapped me. And while he's a vampire, he's not elite. He's not powerful. He's not wealthy. He is not from the life I was raised in or the future I was promised. He is primal and blue-collar and work boots and something dangerous that I don't understand.

And I want him.

The kiss happens before I can decide whether to fight it.

His mouth presses to mine, steady and certain.

For half a second, I freeze, and then the world tilts as heat surges through me like a hurricane. All the fear inside my nerves dissolves into something grounding. *Something safe.*

My fingers curl into his T-shirt, and I kiss him back.

I savor the taste of his mouth. I savor the taste of his lips and tongue. And I press my body tighter against his until I can feel his arousal against my hip.

I'm overwhelmed with a million different emotions, but the one that stands out the most is hunger. Want. *Desire.*

When he pulls away, I'm shaking and breathless and confused.

And when he leaves me locked in the room again, I'm angry. At him. At myself. At how I could kiss this man who took me without permission and still have it be the best thing I've ever experienced in my life.

But, livid or not, it was the *best*.

And I have no idea why.

11

KANE

BLAIR IS ASLEEP. EVEN THROUGH A LOCKED door, even one floor down, I can feel her. My body can tell that her pulse is slower now and her breathing is even and her anger has been dulled by exhaustion.

The bond doesn't shut off just because she's unconscious. If anything, it only hums louder.

Rook sits at the kitchen table, his arms folded and his jaw tight. If vampires actually needed sleep, he'd look like he hasn't slept in days. Kylie is in his bedroom, turned *their* bedroom, and Cal leans against the counter, arms crossed and waiting.

No one speaks at first, but with the way Cal keeps tossing glare-daggers my way, I know I'm going to have to be the one to break the tension. After all, my extracurriculars are the most recent cause.

"There are more casualties." I shrug. "I…well, I killed the men who were there to take Blair."

"Fuck," Rook mutters.

"Shit, Kane." Cal's jaw ticks. "How many?"

"Two," I admit. "Mark and Evan."

"You've got to be fucking kidding me." Cal sighs. "You killed Holland's boys?"

"In my defense, I didn't get to pick who they sent for her, and they technically started it. I just had to finish it."

Rook drags a hand down his face. "Jesus Christ, Kane."

"They were taking her to some piece of shit elite's private hangar so she could fly to his penthouse in New York." I hold both of their gazes. "I couldn't let that happen. Especially when I could tell not a single one of those fucks had any intention of making plans for her to come back from New York. She was either getting used by Damien or taken to the auction, and neither one worked for me."

Cal nods once. "Damien, as in Damien Snow?"

I shrug.

"Well, shit. Somehow it just keeps getting worse."

"It was just two more gofers, you know?" I toss out, trying to add some levity to this very serious, they-want-us-dead situation. "We've still kept the death count to only one hand."

Cal bursts into laughter. "Fucking hell, Kane. Now isn't the time for jokes."

"What?" I flash a smile at him. "I think we've all been really level-headed about the whole thing."

"Level-headed?" Cal tosses back. "Between the three of us, we've killed five of the elites' fuckstains and kidnapped two women. One of which is *blood of the three.*"

I grimace. "Technically, it's two."

Cal's eyes go wide. "She's *blood of the three* too?"

I nod.

Rook barks out a laugh. "Well, I'd say that pretty much does it."

We were already enemies after he took Kylie, but now? We are quite literally enemy number one to any vampire elite from here to New York.

Kylie appears at the threshold of the living room, but she doesn't look panicked or uncertain, even with the newly kidnapped woman in the bedroom upstairs. She walks straight across the room and into Rook's lap like that's where she belongs. Rook's entire body shifts, and he slides his hand around her waist automatically while his chin rests against her shoulder.

She doesn't ask what we're talking about, but I don't miss the way she and Rook are looking at each other. Something silent passes between them, and it's clear their bond is solidified. And more than that, it's really fucking strong.

They don't need to say things out loud to gossip. They can do it in their fucking heads.

"You two are getting really creepy with that silent thing," Cal teases.

Kylie giggles and presses a kiss to the corner of Rook's jaw. He looks down at her like a man whose entire world resides inside her eyes.

Damn. I never thought I'd see the day when my grumpy-as-fuck big brother Rook looked at a woman the way he's looking at her—even a month ago, he was barely tolerable. Now, he's practically starring in commercials for VampireMatch.com.

Eventually, Rook looks back at me, his moony eyes shuttering noticeably. "Okay, so explain to me again how you even came into contact with Blair?"

"You know that event Holland was trying to get Kylie to go to?" I toss out. "Well, we followed the bastard there to scope it out. And it wasn't some networking bullshit like he was selling. It was a preview for the upcoming auction."

Kylie stiffens. "For an auction?"

"Yeah," Cal says. "It's called the Selection. The vampire elite get to buy the human woman of their choice. It's been going on for way too damn long."

Kylie's hand tightens in Rook's shirt, and shock turns the corners of her mouth down. I don't blame her. She was supposed to be there. In fact, there were three men in her driveway that morning trying to make damn sure she attended, and if we hadn't *dispatched* them, they would have.

"We just stayed in the shadows," Cal adds. "Listened."

"Selection's coming up soon, by the way," I chime in. "No official date yet, but it'll be in New York. Apparently, it's all planned, and they give forty-eight-hour notice to keep the secrecy intact."

Rook sighs and runs a hand through his hair. But when Kylie pales, he wraps his arms around her body and holds her closer to his chest.

"They don't know what it really is," I say. "The women preparing for it. Every single one at that event was naïve to the reality."

"They think it's elevation of status. A privilege. They think they're being fucking chosen," Cal adds. "They were calling it *The Choosing Mixer.*"

"Fuck me," Rook mutters. "And yet, they're being sold." His voice is flat. "Anyone we would consider an ally in that room? Any good vamps at all?"

Cal shakes his head immediately. "Not a single fucking one."

"So…how does Blair come into this?" Rook asks, his eyes meeting mine. "I mean, how the fuck did you end up bringing her here?"

"She was there. At the preview." I don't hesitate. "And I could read her intent."

Rook raises a brow.

"She was naïve," I continue. "Excited, even, to be chosen. She had no idea what any of them has planned."

"But as you already said, most of them don't," Rook says evenly.

"Yeah," I admit. "But this one is *mine*. I felt it immediately. She's my destined."

"What are the fucking odds." Rook sighs and shakes his head. "Not only did we take two women they thought belonged to them, but both are *blood of the three*."

I laugh. I can't help it. "We're pretty fucked now. I mean, we were fucked when you took Kylie, but now we're, like, *really* fucked."

"Yeah. All thanks to you two bastards, I've got the elites wanting my head on a silver platter." Cal runs a hand over his mouth and lets out a deep chuckle. "And I don't even have a fated mate by my side to show for it."

I huff a short laugh. "My fated mate is currently locked in my bedroom upstairs because she's trying to escape me. Let's not act like it's all rainbows and sunshine on this side of things."

Kylie grins. "I wasn't exactly nice to Rook at first."

"Pretty sure I deserved it, baby." Rook laughs, pressing a kiss to Kylie's forehead as he does.

"Okay." Cal smirks. "Fair."

"Probably be thankful," I mutter.

Kylie shifts in Rook's lap, studying me. "So, she doesn't understand any of it, then? What really happens there?"

"No," I say. "She doesn't."

"Well, what's done is done, and we can't go back. Still, we need a clear picture. Anything else you need to get off your chest, Kane?" Rook asks. "No extra bodies you forgot to tell us about? No additional women you took without permission?"

"No, dickhead," I say through a laugh. "Nothing else like that."

"You're holding something back." Rook furrows his brow as he looks at me. "What aren't you saying right now?"

"Well…when she's near me," I say slowly, "I don't just read intent. I can stop it."

Cal tilts his head.

"What do you mean?" Rook asks.

"If the intent is reckless. Or naïve. Or coming from fear. I can interrupt it. Well, at least hers."

"Like you interrupted her screams?" Kylie says softly.

I nod.

Rook glances at Kylie again.

They don't speak, but I can tell they are communicating.

"You can hear her," I state. "Like, completely hear her thoughts."

Prior to Kylie, Rook had been able to read minds, but he had to have permission from the person before being able to get inside their head. And it also wasn't that reliable. But right now, it feels like he and Kylie are having a full-blown conversation that no one can hear but them.

"Yes," Rook admits. "And she can hear mine."

"Holy shit," I mutter. "Fated mates is fucking crazy."

"I don't know because I haven't experienced it yet." Cal sighs and runs a hand through his hair. "But I'm a little worried if I do find my fated mate anytime soon, our ship is going to be sailing through some pretty rough waters."

I laugh and walk over to offer Cal a friendly slap to his shoulder. "Who knows? Maybe your fated mate won't be *blood of the three*. Maybe she'll just be a random girl you meet in the grocery store or some shit."

The thought lands heavier than the joke.

"This is when it would be nice to know who the fuck our parents are," Cal mutters. "At least then we'd have a little more info on how we were brought into this world and who our father is."

Rook's jaw tightens slightly. "We'll never fucking know that, Cal," he says flatly. "So don't waste time on it."

He's right. We don't know. We were dropped into foster care before we could remember anything.

"Well, we do know one thing—the elites are going to retaliate," Cal comments. "It's only a matter of time."

Neither Rook nor I say anything, but it's because there's nothing else to say.

We're all fucking in at this point.

Upstairs, Blair shifts in her sleep, and I feel it immediately.

The pull. The certainty. *The bond.*

I know without question why I took her.

And just like Rook said—there's no going back now.

12

BLAIR

I WAKE UP TO SILENCE, BUT UNFORTUNATELY FOR me, it's not the curated silence of a penthouse sixty floors above New York traffic.

This silence is dense and thick and feels like it weighs a thousand pounds.

For a moment, I lie still, staring at the ceiling, trying to remember why it looks wrong.

But it doesn't take long for the endless view of wood to bring me back to reality. Dark beams stretching overhead like something out of a wilderness catalog. The faint scent of pine lingers in the air.

I'm in a *cabin,* like some *Little House on the Prairie* bullshit. I sit up and look out the window, and instantly, I'm hit with the sight of trees because I'm in the freaking forest.

Gross.

My chest tightens as a memory floods back—his hands, his body, the kiss.

That kiss.

No. I shove that thought away immediately. *I will* not *romanticize kissing my freaking kidnapper.*

I swing my legs over the side of the bed, and my bare feet hit the floor. It's cold. "No heated floors?" I mutter to myself. "How do people live like this?"

The walls, the dresser, and the ceiling are all wood. There is no marble or travertine to be seen, and the finishes are cheap, like someone DIY-ed this cabin themselves.

"This is barbaric."

I need to get the hell out of here before I start to smell like pine trees.

I push off the bed and cross to the door, twisting the handle.

It's locked. Because *of course it is.* Because I've been kidnapped and locked in a lumberyard.

I should probably be panicking, but mostly, I'm *insulted.* My family is too wealthy for me to be stuck inside a wilderness cabin. My father is one of the richest men in our circle. He knows senators and CEOs. He has private security on speed dial. If I don't show up in New York, people will notice. If I don't call, if I don't check in, there will be questions.

There will be action.

There will be a search.

There *has* to be.

I lift my chin slightly at the thought.

They'll find me. They'll trace the SUV he was driving. Surely our cameras caught his license plate. They'll have the whole damn Boston police force out looking for me and might even call in the army.

This won't last long. I'll be rescued soon.

My gaze drifts to the window again, and all I find is an endless sea of trees. There are no roads or rooftops or neighboring estates. Just forest as far as the eye can see.

Immediately, my confidence falters.

We are in the middle of nowhere. Even if there is a search party, what are they searching? Miles of wilderness?

My stomach twists, but I refuse to fall to pieces. *Windsor women do not fall to pieces*, my mother would say. *Windsor women are strong and confident and can handle anything.*

I turn away from the window, and when I spot the bathroom, I make the decision to salvage some normalcy. I'll take a shower. That will make me feel better. That will help me figure out how to get out of this hellhole.

I flick on the light, revealing a clean but painfully simple space. Again. It's like the Dark Ages. There is no marble or gold fixtures or oversized mirrors. No lush bath towels or robes. Just plastic bullshit like a bathroom is meant for efficiency instead of luxury.

Clearly, the importance of self-care is not understood around here.

If only Kidnapper Kane had had the decency to toss my suitcase in his stupid SUV when he took me, I'd have everything I need to complete my twenty-step skincare routine and daily hair conditioning regimen. *At least then, I'd have my doll.*

There mere thought of my most beloved possession makes tears prick my eyes, but I blink them away fast. I will *not* cry. I will not show weakness. I'm a Windsor woman, for fuck's sake, and Windsor women are strong.

When I turn on the shower and remove my clothes, I catch

sight of the singular bottle inside the tub—*yes, a freaking tub for a shower*. I pick it up and stare at the words, **three-in-one**.

A shocked laugh escapes my throat. "Is this a joke?" I whisper as I read the rest of the label that showcases **shampoo, conditioner**, and **body wash** all combined into one product.

They make this? And people buy it?

Honestly, the marketing idea that the needs of hair and skin are the same should be categorized as a hate crime.

I exhale a deep sigh before stepping into the shower with the stupid bottle. The water pressure is fine, but not perfect. And I resign myself to using one product to wash my body, my hair, and my face.

I can already feel my skin drying out. Good grief. I'm certain cavemen had better products than this. Once I'm done and step out, I wrap my body in one of the pathetically itchy bath towels and start searching for hair products and a hair dryer.

All the drawers are empty, save a hairbrush. No hair dryer. No serums. No face masks. No leave-in hair conditioner.

All I have is a brush and a freaking towel.

People actually live like this?

On a huff, I rub my hair aggressively with the towel, watching it frizz in the mirror. And after I run a brush through it, I have to…leave it…as is.

My mom would be horrified to know I'm going to spend an entire day in this state. I already look younger and softer and… *ordinary*.

The word makes my throat tighten. I was never meant to be ordinary.

I am special. I was raised to be chosen.

And every lesson, every event, every introduction to powerful people in my parents' inner circle carefully positioned me toward that future. It was possible that Damien Snow was the next step in the plan. That New York was just the beginning of all my dreams and everything my mother had worked so hard for.

But I'm not in New York.

I'm here, inside a cabin in the wilderness after being kidnapped by a vampire who repossesses cars for a living.

God help me.

I let out a sharp breath and march back into the bedroom, opening the dresser in search of something to wear. Of course, all I find are men's clothes—flannels, T-shirts, jeans, *sweatpants.*

What the hell is happening right now?!

I slam the drawer shut and start pacing.

"How in the hell did I end up here?" I whisper to myself, anger vibrating from my voice. "I shouldn't be here. I should be in New York with Damien or, at the very least, at home."

For all I know, they've already given the forty-eight-hour notice, and all the other girls are heading to New York for the Choosing Ceremony too.

Tears prick my eyes, and I swallow hard against the knot in my throat. *I will not cry. I will not freaking cry. Windsor women do not cry.*

"This is temporary," I reassure myself. "It will be fixed. Daddy will find a way to fix this. He'll find me. They'll find me."

I move to the door and press my ear against it, but I don't hear any footsteps or voices or signs of *him.* My chest tightens, and my mouth turns down at the corners, and I instantly become irritated with myself.

Why do I care where he is?

Rationalizing, I keep my composure because *Windsors keep their poise.* I just need to know where the threat is. That's all.

My gaze drifts to the wall beside the bed, and a memory creeps back in uninvited.

His mouth on mine last night.

The way my anger dissolved.

The way my fear shifted into something warmer and safer.

I press my lips together hard. *That was just shock and adrenaline and trauma, Blair.*

It was not—

I close my eyes briefly, and I can still feel it. The heat of his body. The steadiness of his muscles. The way my body leaned into him like it recognized something before my mind did.

"I do not want him. I *hate* him," I whisper, but the words feel lean. And the realization unsettles me far more than the cold floors or the missing marble or the three-in-one body wash.

I shouldn't want to see him. He kidnapped me. He killed people. He is holding me here in this cabin against my will.

And yet, this room feels emptier without him in it.

Which is the most disturbing thought of all.

Obviously, I'm delirious and tired and probably in shock still.

Soon, someone will come rescue me.

And if they don't?

I'll have to find a way to escape.

13

KANE

She hasn't eaten.

Now it's late afternoon, and the cabin has gone quiet in that heavy way it does when everyone is trying not to think too loudly. Rook and Kylie are downstairs in their room. Cal is in the small garage that's connected to the cabin. And I'm busy trying to find a way to get Blair to not starve out of spite.

I'm no chef—I don't need to fucking eat, so I don't need to fucking cook—but I make something simple with painstaking effort and care. I go with grilled cheese and tomato soup, hoping it's something light and doesn't ask too much of her stomach, as well as figuring it's hard to mess up bread and cheese and something out of a can. It's highly likely it's not up to par with the luxury meals Blair Windsor is used to her family's live-in chef making, but I'll have to save the duck confit for later in my food preparation timeline.

Rich-girl problems, you know?

Having grown up in foster care, I wouldn't know shit about being rich, but I'm not going to judge her for not understanding what it's like to grow up blue-collar. She's been sheltered her whole fucking life. Fed with a golden spoon. Taught to view the world through a skewed lens of privilege and wealth.

I already overheard her quietly bitching to herself about my lack of skin products and choice in body wash while she was taking a shower, which was amusing, to say the least. If she weren't trying to hate me so much, I'd be tempted to offer to eat her pussy to make up for the soap travesty—a skill at which I'm already an expert.

But I'm resigning myself to keeping things simple and not fantasizing about all the things I want to do to Blair Windsor's body—taste, lick, suck, fuck, *worship*—before I've even been checked into the game.

I'm a benchwarmer for now, plain and simple.

I carry the plate of food upstairs and head to my bedroom. The last thing I want to do is startle her, so when I unlock the door, I don't rush in. I step inside slowly, like the air itself might fracture if I move too fast.

She's fast asleep and curled on her side in bed, and she's dressed in nothing but my T-shirt. The shirt hangs loose on her small frame—one shoulder slipping slightly out of the neckline and the hem brushing the middle of her thighs. And her hair is still faintly damp from the shower I heard her take earlier, the ends curling lightly against my pillow.

Fuck me. Her in my bed. My shirt on her body. It's a gorgeous sight, and I have to make a conscious effort not to fixate on it too much.

I close the door quietly behind me and set the tray down on the nightstand without taking my eyes off her. She looks smaller asleep. Less sharp. Less furious. There's no outrage in her face now, just softness and beauty and relaxed breaths.

The mattress dips slightly under my weight as I sit on the edge of the bed.

Her brows twitch. Then—without waking—she shifts toward me.

Her knee brushes my hip. Her hand drifts across the mattress until her fingers graze my thigh. Her body follows the contact instinctively, curling closer as if she's been searching for heat.

The bond pulls tight in my chest.

I should move. I should stand back up. I should leave the bedroom.

Instead, I slowly lie down beside her.

The second I settle into the mattress, she presses into me fully. Her forehead tucks beneath my chin. Her fingers curl into the fabric at my waist. Her leg slides between mine like it belongs there.

It's unconscious and just as necessary for her as it is for me. That's what undoes me.

She hates me when she's awake. But in sleep, when she's completely relaxed and not overthinking every fucking thing she's ever been told, she's drawn to me like a magnet.

It's the confirmation I need to know that, despite the rocky path ahead, I've made the right choice. Our bond is important to me, but it's important to her too—it's our destined future.

My arm slides around her before I can stop it. My palm settles at the curve of her back, feeling the steady rhythm of her breathing beneath the thin cotton.

She almost went to New York. Almost walked straight into Damien Snow's evil hands. Straight into a cage dressed up as luxury.

The thoughts cut through me sharply.

The things he would've done to her. The cruel intentions that lay beneath the surface of his plans.

Fuck. I have to close my eyes to keep my rage and anger under control.

I know with certainty I would burn that whole fucking city to the ground before I let him touch her. She is *my* fated mate. I know I'm hers and she is mine, but I'll never force her to choose me.

Never. The mere thought is abhorrent to me. *I love her too much.* When Blair gives in to our bond, it'll be because she chooses it.

She stirs and her breathing changes, and between one heartbeat and the next, her lashes flutter open.

I brace for impact. For the shove. The slap. The fury.

But she doesn't recoil. Her eyes are open, but they're unfocused and soft around the edges. She's here, but she also isn't fully awake. This is a layer just below consciousness where the secrets live.

"I hate that I want to kiss you again," she whispers, her voice still drowsy with sleep.

Her words hit me low and hard and threaten to awaken my primal need for her.

"Blair," I murmur quietly.

But she's already moving. She slides her hand up my chest, fingers tracing muscle like she's confirming I'm real.

Then her mouth is on mine. Her lips are soft and searching, and for a second, I don't respond. I let her decide.

She makes a frustrated sound against my lips when I hesitate, and then she shifts her weight, climbing over me in one fluid motion until she's straddling me.

Her hair falls forward, brushing my face. The warmth of her body over mine sends a violent surge of heat through me. My hands come up instinctively to steady her at her waist.

She kisses me harder. Her body coming at mine with a hungry, desperate edge that takes every ounce of willpower I have to keep myself in check. To stay restrained. To not give in to how badly I fucking need her.

My cock is hard beneath the zipper of my jeans, and she grinds herself against me.

"Blair," I say softly, warning threaded through her name.

She doesn't slow. She just keeps kissing me and grinding against me, and her fingers tangle in my hair. She tastes like fucking heaven, and she feels soft beneath my hands. *I want her. I need her. I love her.*

She kisses me deeper, harder, and the invisible string connecting us tugs so hard I feel the pull in my spine. My body demands I take her, claim her, anchor her to me permanently.

I won't. I *can't.* Not before she lets go of the need to hate me.

She moves her hands to the hem of the shirt she's wearing—my shirt—and she starts to lift it.

Fuck. I have to stop this.

That's when I move. I roll us carefully, flipping her onto her back in one smooth motion. Not rough or dominant but controlled.

Her hair fans across the pillow, her lips part, and her eyes are still that distant, dream-hazed blue.

I lower my mouth to hers again, but slower now. I kiss her

like something fragile, taking the tension from hunger and desperation to soft and gentle.

I slide my hand into her hair, smoothing it back from her face. I trail my fingers down her arm, over her wrist, and back up again. I move slow and steady and in a rhythm that relaxes her.

Her breathing shifts, and she sighs softly against my mouth.

I kiss her cheek. Her jaw. The corner of her lips. And with each soft press of my mouth, the tight grip her hands have on my shirt begins to loosen.

Her body melts into the mattress beneath me. The tension drains from her limbs. A few more kisses and her lashes lower until her eyes are closed.

And a few more kisses after that and her body fully relaxes until she's asleep again.

I stay there a moment longer, hovering over her, until I roll onto my back beside her.

The ceiling beams blur slightly as I stare up at them. My cock is still hard, and every inch of my body aches with want.

"Fuck," I mutter under my breath.

She trusts me in her sleep. She reaches for me when she isn't thinking. But when she wakes, she'll remember who she thinks she's supposed to be.

I turn my head and look at her again, studying every facet of her being. Her dark hair, her long lashes, and the curve of her soft jaw. Her body is still curled toward mine, and she looks so beautifully peaceful.

I want to be the man who gets to make her look like that forever—and I will, eventually. She's mine. I know that with every ounce of my body.

But war is also coming. The elites are undoubtedly working to track us down, and happily ever after may have a time limit.

I need to make her mine on a cellular level that no one could ever refute, give us a slight advantage, but I can't rush just to beat the clock.

I can't force the bond to make myself stronger, and I can't force Blair to trust me.

I'll have to take this war as it comes. Even if it kills me.

14

WAKE UP WITH MY HEART RACING.

I sit up too fast, scanning the room like something might have changed overnight, but nothing has. I'm still in this stupid fucking ugly cabin because I've been kidnapped by some blue-collar repo man vampire.

Ugh. This is such bullshit.

The side of the bed beside me is empty and cold. Kane, my kidnapper, is nowhere in sight.

I swing my legs over the edge and cross the room in quick strides, grabbing the door handle.

Locked.

I turn slowly toward the bed, and my eyes rake over the rumpled sheets on both sides of the mattress. My stomach twists into a knot with uninvited warmth and memories.

Was he in here?

I step toward the pillow on his side of the bed, and before I can stop myself, I press my face into it. Instantly, I'm hit with the scent of him—inviting, masculine, distinct—it's an aroma that, for some strange reason, I *know* as though it's my own.

He was in here, while I was sleeping. I remember sharply, as though I wasn't asleep at all.

His body beside mine. My leg sliding between his. My mouth on his. The way I climbed over him.

I jerk back from the pillow like it's burned me.

No freaking way. That had to have been a dream.

It *had* to be.

I might be delirious from being, you know, kidnapped, but there is no way in hell I'd straddle my abductor and kiss him like I was starving. I press my fingers to my lips, bent on proving my theory, but to my utter dismay, they feel tender and slightly bruised.

"Oh my God," I whisper. "Did I kiss him…again?"

My mind starts to race. *Is this what happens to victims? Do they start sympathizing with the person who took them? Is this some twisted survival response where my brain is rewriting him into something safe?*

I pace the room, dragging my fingers through my already dried-out hair.

I stop in front of the mirror and stare. My face is devoid of makeup, my cheeks rosy but not from blush, and my hair is frizzing at the ends and flattening at the crown.

I look stripped fucking bare.

"Wow," I mutter. "Pretty sure this is the worst I've looked in my entire life."

I was raised to be polished and sophisticated and presentable. Not frizzy and unkempt and a complete dumpster fire.

I throw myself down onto the bed in frustration.

But not even a minute later, I hear the sound of the lock clicking, and I sit up immediately.

The door opens, and a girl who looks like she could be my

age, maybe a year or two older, walks in carrying a plate of toast and scrambled eggs.

She's wearing a soft sweater and jeans and not an ounce of designer anything on her body. She looks normal. She looks… boring. Well, besides her face and her hair. Both are beautiful in a way that makes me annoyed.

She pauses when she sees me watching her. "Hi, Blair," she says gently. "I'm Kylie."

"Do you know you're in a cabin with a vampire?"

A small laugh escapes her. "Yes. Better than that, there are three vampire men in this cabin."

Three? Holy hell. I knew there were others, but I had no idea that brought the total to three vampires and a human woman.

"Why are you here?" I ask, dropping my voice to a whisper. "Are you being held against your will too?"

"No. I'm not being held against my will. Kane's brother Rook is my…" She hesitates. "Well, I guess the only word that will make sense to you right now is probably husband."

"Kane has a brother?" He's not some kind of loner, family-less psychopath like I've been picturing?

"He has two," she continues. "Rook and Calloway."

"What do they do?" I ask. "Besides being accomplices in the kidnapping of a woman."

"Rook's a garbage man," she says easily. "Calloway's a mechanic. He also does demolition work."

"Wait…" I stare at her. "You married a garbage man?"

There's no edge to her voice when she responds. "Yes."

I open my mouth, but nothing comes out. Honestly, the idea is so foreign I don't know how to respond. Blue-collar men were background noise in my life. They fixed things and they left. They didn't sit at dinner tables. Even the staff that lives at my parents' house always keeps to themselves and stays out of our way for the most part.

Besides my nanny, I never had much interaction with, like, normal people. *Nanny Celeste, the only person who ever let me cry without correcting my posture.*

I haven't seen or talked to her since I was eighteen. When Bonnie and I got old enough not to need a nanny anymore—ten-year-olds should be capable of independence, according to my parents—and only needed a driver, she left us to start working for another family with two small boys.

And you still miss her because she was more of a mother to you than—

I cut off the thought before it can grow legs and run.

"Rook saved my life," Kylie says, her voice soft and quiet in ways that threaten to knock down my guard.

"What do you mean?"

"I mean, I was moments away from being kidnapped, and he saved me," she admits. "This man named Holland had sent three men to collect me from my own house."

"Holland?" I question.

"Yes. Holland Thorne."

My hands start to shake. "How do you know Holland Thorne?"

"I ice-skate…well, I used to ice-skate at this rink where he played hockey. Where Rook and Kane and Calloway played hockey too."

Kane plays hockey? That's so…violent. *Mind you, you saw him kill two men…*

"You know Holland too?" Kylie asks.

"Yeah, and he's actually a super-nice guy, so I highly doubt he sent men to your freaking house to kidnap you."

"Is he super-nice, though?" she questions. "I know he is on the surface, but deep down?"

"What are you trying to say?" I question. "That Holland is some kind of monster? I've been around him since I was a teenager. I think if he were evil, like you say, I'd know it."

"People have a way of surprising us," she says. "He came across as nice to me too, for a while. He wanted me to go to an event with him last Friday, and I thought I had the choice, but in reality, he was going to force me to go whether I wanted to or not."

"Wait…he wanted you to go to the Choosing Mixer?" I laugh. "I highly doubt that. I mean, no offense. But that's only for…*special* women."

"Special women who are of the right bloodline? *Blood of the three*, right?"

My jaw gapes open. "How do you know about that?"

"Because my mother was *blood of the three*. And I am too."

I narrow my eyes and look her up and down before I can stop myself. "But you're not, like, rich. I mean, no offense, but it's pretty clear in your choice of clothing."

"No, I'm not rich." She shrugs, completely unfazed by the dig. Her family must have blown all their dowries or something. "And technically, I didn't even know vampires existed before Rook saved me." She searches my face. "And Kane saved your life too. Even if you don't realize that yet. He did."

"You think Kane saved my life?" I scoff. "Do you even understand how insane that sounds? You're talking about the man who killed two men in my driveway and dragged me into some cabin in the woods against my will."

"Yeah, you're right, but he stopped something worse."

"There is no worse," I retort. "He kept me from going to New York. I was supposed to spend time with an elite vampire there. An elite vampire who was probably going to choose *me* over all the other women available."

"The vampire elite are not what you think they are, Blair. My mother and father were *killed* by the vampire elite. They're rich, but they aren't well-intentioned. Not even close."

Her words hit like a slap, and I jerk my head back in shock. "Don't lie about shit like that. It's not funny."

"I'm not lying."

"My mom has prepared me my entire life to be chosen," I say, my voice sharpening. "She would not do that if they were dangerous. The elite have been in my home since I was a child. They came to my birthday parties. They attended my parents' yearly Christmas party. I know them *personally*. Just because they have money and power, that doesn't make them monsters."

Kylie doesn't argue. She just watches me, which somehow feels worse.

"I'm one of the lucky ones," I continue. "You don't understand how this works. Being chosen is an honor."

"I understand that's what they've told you, but what if they lied? What if being chosen isn't what you think it is, Blair?"

I shake my head. "You have no idea what you're talking about. My father walks inside the inner circle. I've been around them my entire life. I know these men."

"But do you really *know* them? Have you been around the

women they've chosen previously? Do they parade them around and shower them with gifts?"

Her question pushes against something in my head, reminding me of the text conversation I had with Holland before I was supposed to go to New York and how secret and secluded it was all supposed to be. I've barely ever seen the men my dad knows with a woman, but it was business. Of course they wouldn't be there.

"Yes. I do know them."

She doesn't press. She holds my gaze.

And suddenly, the cabin feels smaller.

"You know what? I think I'm done with this bullshit," I say through gritted teeth. "Either help me get out of this ugly cabin," I say coldly, "or get out of my prison room."

The words hang between us for a good twenty seconds before Kylie nods once.

"Okay," she says softly. "I'll leave you to adapt on your own. But just know, I'm here if you need anything. I could help you if you let me. Believe it or not, I understand."

After that, she turns and walks out the door. She wants to paint herself as a friend, but I don't miss the fact that the outside lock clicks back into place after the door is closed.

Silence settles back in, and I sit on the edge of the bed, trying to steady my breaths.

Being chosen isn't what you think it is, her words repeat in my head.

I press my palms against my eyes.

It's ridiculous. It has to be. Because if it isn't...

Then my entire life has been a lie.

15

KANE

THE LATE-MORNING LIGHT BLEEDS THROUGH THE narrow cabin windows, showcasing the particles of dust floating in the beams, and the second night of being a kidnapper has officially passed. On the couch, Kylie is drinking a cup of coffee, tucked into Rook's side, and Cal sits across from them.

Blair is upstairs, locked inside my bedroom, and still asleep in my bed.

"Are you ready to hear the good news or the bad news?" Cal tosses out. For the past twelve hours, he's been on a surveillance run, trying to get ahold of any intel he could. We'd prefer not to be sitting ducks if the elites have sniffed out this cabin and are planning on knocking down our fucking door.

"Honestly, I'm surprised there's even good news," I joke to lighten the mood, and Rook snorts. Truth be told, if Cal is saying there's bad news, that means it's pretty fucking bad.

"Let's hear the good news first," Rook comments.

"They haven't sniffed out the cabin yet," Cal updates. "They have no idea we're here."

"But they're looking for us," I say, and he nods.

"*Hunting* us," Cal corrects. "They hit up Concordia…"

Rook raises an eyebrow. "And?"

"They destroyed everything," Cal answers through a firm jaw. "My house, my shop, both of your places, it was burned to a crisp after they ransacked all of our shit."

"Well, that's a real kick to the balls," I comment and scrub a hand down my face. "Though, I know I shouldn't be surprised. It's the whole reason we came out here in the first place."

"I guess it's a good fucking thing we've all been hoarding cash since we turned eighteen," Rook acknowledges. Real talk, the three of us aren't rich like the fucking elites, but our experiences in foster care instilled at an early age never to count on anyone but ourselves.

And when we got jobs and started living on our own, that mentality stuck with us. Between the three of us, we could stay out here in this cabin for the next sixty years and be fine. Now, that lifestyle doesn't include fucking private chefs and staff and drivers like Blair's, but when material shit doesn't matter to you, it's a satisfying way to live.

"Welp." I huff out a laugh. "I guess it's also a good thing we learned early on not to stuff it in some bank account we could be traced to either. Almost as if we've been preparing our whole adult lives for this. I mean, fuck, we even purchased this land with aliases. It's kind of crazy when I think back on it."

"Yeah." Rook looks down at Kylie, and I don't miss the way his whole fucking heart is in his eyes. "Fate is smarter than we are. Though, that's not a surprise. The shocking part is that she chose us as a vessel."

As I laugh at his joke, Kylie just snuggles into him further, unwilling to interrupt us but wanting to be close to her mate.

When I watch the two of them together, it only makes my chest ache with the need to have that very same thing with Blair. She's my whole fucking world, even if she keeps trying to convince herself to hate me.

"What about Blair?" I ask Cal. "Did you stop in Boston?"

"I did." He shakes his head and runs a hand through his hair. "And I didn't hear a single fucking peep."

I furrow my brow. "What do you mean?"

"I mean, her family is going about their lives as if it's business as usual. Her face isn't plastered on a missing persons poster or showcased on the national news. There isn't a grid search or a town meet point. It's as if she isn't missing at all."

My jaw drops, offended. I may be the fuck who took her, but I'd sure as shit have the grace to be concerned if I were the one she was taken from. "What the fuck? Why aren't they trying to find their freaking daughter? I dropped two bodies in their driveway. I didn't clean up. I left their car and everything."

"I don't know yet." He shakes his head. "But I'll keep trying to find out."

If Blair knew that her family was just living their lives like normal, I know it would break her fucking heart.

Rook meets my eyes. "Are you going to tell her?"

"No." I shake my head. "Not yet. Not until we have more intel."

Cal starts to talk about the logistics of where he went and what conversations he overheard, but my mind is drawn upstairs when I can feel her waking up in my bed. I pull the key to my bedroom out of my pocket and stare down at it.

"So, you don't think we need to relocate?" Rook asks Cal.

"No," Cal responds, but then a self-deprecating laugh escapes his throat. "But also, where would we go?"

"I don't fucking kno—"

"This isn't working," I cut Rook off.

"Huh?" Rook tilts his head to the side. "What isn't?"

"Locking Blair in."

Silence stretches across the room, and Cal studies me closely. "You think letting her roam free is a better idea?"

"She's not a fucking animal," I snap, more heat than I mean to put behind it. "Sorry," I quickly apologize because, fuck, I don't want to be an asshole to them. I'm the one who created this mess. "I just…don't feel right about keeping her locked up. She deserves better than that."

And after finding out that her fucking family isn't even looking for her, I simply can't let her be up there by herself. No matter how stubborn and obstinate she can be, she deserves love and care. She deserves to be a part of our family, even if she doesn't think she wants to be.

"I think you're right, Kane," Kylie agrees. She shifts slightly in Rook's arms, sitting up to look at me. "When I talked to her yesterday, she tried to act strong, but it was obvious to me she's scared. And confused. And…I'm sure being locked up isn't helping her come to any important realizations."

"I know." I scrub a hand over my face. "It's not fair to her. Frankly, the fact that her parents were happy to send her off to an evil bloodsucker who was fully prepared to…" I pause, unable to even say the words to describe the horrible, vile things he planned. "I just can't be this guy, you know? I'm not this guy. It goes against the reasons we're on this side of the fight altogether."

I can feel Blair upstairs. But then again, I can *always* feel her. The bond is constant, always humming low and steady inside my chest.

Right now, she's fully awake and pacing and agitated. But she isn't plotting or scheming on how to escape like she was yesterday. She's unraveling.

"I don't want to cage her," I say, more to myself than anyone else. "Not like this."

"Okay." Cal crosses his arms over his chest. "So, what's the plan, then?"

"Daylight freedom," I answer, and I hate that I still have to put stipulations on what she can and can't do. No one deserves that, but fuck, she's a flight risk. A flight risk that will unknowingly put herself in the worst kind of situation because her whole entire life has revolved around telling her "being chosen" by an elite vampire is a good thing. "Perimeter only. She doesn't go past the tree line. One of us is always outside with her."

Rook holds my stare for a beat, then nods once. "Your call," he says. "But if she runs—"

"She won't," I say automatically.

It's a lie. Even I know it's a lie. There's a strong likelihood that Blair will try to run, but I refuse to be the bastard who keeps her locked up in a room twenty-four hours a day.

I head for the stairs before I can overthink it. The second-floor hallway is quiet, and sunlight cuts through the narrow window at the end of it, turning the wooden floor pale gold.

I stop outside the bedroom door.

For a second, I just stand there, listening.

Her footsteps cross the room. Then stop. Then start again. She's so restless, she's going to pace holes into the floorboards if I let this insanity continue.

Yeah. I refuse to keep her locked up like this.

The key slides into the lock, and the click sounds louder than it should.

Inside, everything goes still.

I open the door to find Blair standing near the window, her arms folded tightly across her chest. Her hair is loose down her back, and despite her current situation, she looks polished and confident, like she was born knowing how to hold herself upright, no matter the setting.

Her eyes flick to mine.

"I'm unlocking the door."

Her posture shifts almost imperceptibly. She's suspicious at first, but then a few quiet moments later, her shoulders soften. "Why?" she asks.

"Because I don't want to cage you," I answer honestly. "I just want to keep you safe."

The words hang between us.

"So…" She pauses, and she tilts her head to the side as she assesses my face. "You're going to let me out of this room?"

"Yes."

"I can go anywhere inside and outside?"

"There are boundaries," I add calmly. "You stay within the cabin perimeter. You don't cross the tree line. One of us is always outside with you."

Her lips press into a thin line. "So, you're not keeping me caged, but you're not exactly giving me full freedom."

I shrug. "I wish I could. But I don't trust the people who would take advantage of that freedom."

"And you're not worried about me trying to escape?"

"You won't."

Her eyes flash at that. "You're very confident."

"Well, I have an unfair advantage when it comes to you," I say quietly. "And I know you don't want to stay locked in here."

"Unfair advantage?" Her pulse jumps at my words, thrumming quickly at her neck. "What does that mean?"

Intention, Blair. I can read your intention. Hell, I am so fucking locked in on you I can tell when you're awake or asleep or worrying yourself sick about shampoo. I can feel your emotions from miles away.

But I don't tell her that. In fact, I don't answer at all.

She stares at me, her pretty blue eyes trying to read my face.

I know she hates the confinement. She hates feeling powerless, but no matter how badly she wants to hate me, she can't. Most of the time, when I'm not near, her intentions are mixed with her wondering where I am and what I'm doing.

"No matter what you've been raised to think about vampires," I eventually say, "I'm not the type of vampire that wants to treat you like property, Blair. That never has and never will be my intention."

Her expression falters just slightly.

"I won't cage you," I say again, slower this time. "But I won't let you walk into danger either."

Silence stretches as she studies me like she's trying to figure out what the angle is and where the manipulation lies.

She won't find either. My heart is bare with her.

Finally, she walks past me toward the open door. Her body is close enough that her shoulder brushes mine as she pauses in the doorway.

The contact sends a low current through me.

"If I'm not your prisoner," she says without looking at me, "then why do you want to bother with keeping me here? Why do you even care what happens to me?"

"Because you're not just something to me, Blair. You're fucking everything," I say the truth because it's all I have. "And though I don't own you, you *are* mine."

Her breath stutters, and her eyes search mine for a long moment. She's tempted to step back toward me; I can feel the need vibrating through her body.

But eventually, she forces herself to avert her eyes from mine, blinks several times, and then she steps into the hallway.

I follow her lead to the main floor and watch in amusement as Blair descends the stairs like she's entering a ballroom instead of a cabin kitchen, taking in the room without turning her head too much.

My brother Rook follows her closely with studious caution.

Calloway leans back casually with an entertained grin on his lips. The bastard has already made up his mind that she's going to run the second she has the chance and is probably intrigued to watch me chase after her.

"Good morning, Blair." Thankfully, Kylie is her usual friendly and sweet self, which breaks up the monotony of three very intimidating, imposingly figured vampires.

"Good morning," Blair says, and she doesn't hesitate to walk to the table and sit down. "I'll eat," she adds, as if she's granting us all something by not only gracing us with her presence but letting us feed her too.

Rook looks over at me like, *who the fuck does your chick think she is?*

Cal chuckles to himself.

I laugh out loud. I can't help it. Blair Windsor is unlike any woman I've ever met in my life. Only she could get kidnapped and demand food from her captors.

"You're in luck because I just made some breakfast," Kylie says and moves to the table with a plate of eggs and toast.

Once the food is in front of her, Blair picks up the fork and takes a small bite.

"Scrambled eggs, okay?" Kylie asks.

"It's…fine," Blair says.

Rook huffs quietly, unamused by anyone who shows Ky anything less than the utmost respect.

Both Kylie and Cal hide their grins.

I don't take my eyes off Blair. Underneath the calm facade, I feel her intentions. Not rebellion but something coiled. She's making a genuine effort, but she's also bracing for impact.

Fuck me. I hate how right she is to feel poised for the next blow. This shit is so far from over, it's not even funny.

The urge to walk over to her and wrap her up in my arms is almost too much to bear. But I force myself to play it cool, to give her space, to not push for too much, no matter how badly the need to comfort her overwhelms my senses.

She glances up. Our eyes lock. And for a split second, the storm inside her body quiets. Because the bond is growing stronger by the day. That's how it works. The more proximity there is, the more intense it will become, outside factors be damned.

Her shoulders lower and relax as she continues to eat the plate of food Kylie gave her. Right now, she feels safe, even if it's confusing for her. And I can imagine she fucking hates that the only time her pulse steadies is when I'm near, even if I get a real thrill from it.

I move closer to the table. I don't touch her, but I stand next to her chair. "You're free to move around," I say evenly. "Daylight only. Stay within sight of the cabin."

She rolls her eyes, but she also nods. "Yes, sir. Mr. Kidnapper."

Kylie snorts. Rook grins. And Cal doesn't hold back his laugh.

Hell, I don't hold back mine either.

And for the first time since I brought her to this cabin, she smiles at me. It's not trust or forgiveness, but it's something close to relief.

Fuck, it's a beautiful sight.

And I hope it's the start of a shift inside her.

16

DAY THREE OF BEING AT THE SLATER BROTHERS' cabin and the first thing I notice when I wake up is the door isn't locked. In fact, it's cracked open.

For a long moment, I stare at it. And when I sit up, I half expect it to click shut again as if yesterday was some kind of mistake.

But it doesn't.

Instantly, Kane's words fill my head. *I don't want to cage you. I just want to keep you safe.*

I swing my legs off the bed and stand, smoothing my hands down the borrowed oversized sweater I'm wearing. It isn't mine. None of this is mine. But Lord knows I wouldn't surround myself with wood-paneled walls and plastic bathtubs by choice. I'd also choose a different scent besides cedar and pine to assault my nostrils with on a daily freaking basis.

Vanilla, anyone? A little lavender, perhaps? *Sheesh.*

But when I walk into the bathroom to pee and brush my teeth, I just about trip over my feet when I spot brand-new products on the sink. A hair dryer, a straightener, face wash, separate shampoo and conditioner and body wash, lip gloss, blush, mascara, makeup brushes…there are so many new things, they practically take up the entire counter.

And beside the items sits a little note scribbled in very masculine handwriting.

> I wasn't sure what you needed, so I got everything I could find. I hope it helps make things more comfortable for you.
>
> -Kane

I run my finger over two of the bottles—face moisturizer and toner.

He got me toner?

When I look up at my reflection in the mirror, I'm *smiling*. And when a visual of Kane's green eyes and his full lips starts to form behind my eyes, I have to make a concerted effort not to take it any further.

This is *thoughtful*. It's personal. And while the real nag about my missing suitcase with *my* stuff—*and my doll*—still thrums deep, I can't be angry with him for trying.

I hop in the shower and then use every single product and appliance on that counter. By the time I'm finished, despite the depressing wardrobe of flannel and sweatpants, my hair is shiny and my lips are glossy and my eyes are highlighted by mascara. I almost feel like myself again.

I step into the hall, and I expect Kane to be standing guard outside the door, but a little pit of disappointment forms in my belly when he's not.

I walk to the end of the hall, and the stairs creak under my feet as I descend to the main area below. My eyes scan the kitchen first, and I find Rook standing behind Kylie with one hand braced on the counter near her hip. I swear, it's like the man doesn't know how to exist without touching her or something.

Calloway is rinsing something in the sink.

I frown, looking around the room again.

But just before I can open my mouth to ask where Kane is, the kitchen door swings open, and he steps inside with several blocks of wood in his arms.

His eyes meet mine, and my heart skips a beat.

Stupid heart.

"Morning, Blair," he says, a warm smile on his full lips.

"Good morning," I greet, and for some strange reason, a surge of nerves floats around inside my belly. "So…thanks for all the… stuff."

"You're welcome." He winks. And goodness, I don't know why that wink is so sexy, but it is.

He walks past me to drop the wood near the fireplace, and his scent somehow manages to overpower the pine and cedar so much that my head swims in it. Flannel, cotton, earth, and something kind of spicy and sweet—it's mind-blowing that I would think that combination smells good.

I mean, have you ever been to The Plaza in New York and gotten a whiff of what they're pumping into the air there? It's heaven.

Not quite as heavenly as Kane, though.

A half cough, half laugh escapes Kylie's big, broody vampire man, and I glance over my shoulder to find him looking at me.

"What?" I question with narrowed eyes.

And the bastard just smiles at me. "Didn't say anything."

I don't miss the way he and Kylie make goo-goo ga-ga eyes at each other, and I let out an annoyed huff as I follow Kane's lead into the kitchen.

But when I realize I'm following him like some kind of lost puppy, I redirect myself to the kitchen table and plop down in one of the wooden chairs instead.

"Blair, do you like soup?" Kylie asks, and I look across the room to meet her eyes.

"Soup?"

"Yeah." Kylie smiles. *Goodness, she's insanely pretty, and she doesn't have an ounce of makeup on her face.*

"Um…sure?" I shrug. "Doesn't everyone like soup?"

"I don't," Kane chimes in, waggling his brows. "Never been much for food, you know?"

I laugh. I can't help it. But then I quickly clamp my lips shut when I realize I'm having a little too much fun with him. The last thing I need is to get attached to my captor.

Yet here you are, trying to follow him around like a puppy.

Rook does that weird choking laugh thing again, and Kylie just smacks his shoulder playfully. "Stop being annoying."

He grins at her. "Who? Me?"

"Yes, you," she responds and presses a kiss to his lips. "Now, if you don't mind, I'm going to start on my gammy's famous beef vegetable soup." She looks at me. "Do you want to help, Blair?"

Help? As in, help? *Like what maids and staff do?*

I have never helped in a kitchen before. There were always people for that. Hell, I don't even know if I've ever seen my mom in the actual kitchen besides when she was meal-planning with our chefs.

Kylie looks at me like she just asked the simplest question in the world, and I don't know what else to do besides nod.

"Sure." I shrug one shoulder. "Why the hell not. Not like there's anything else to do around here."

Kane laughs at my words, and I don't hesitate to flip him the middle finger.

But it only makes him laugh more. "You're real fucking cute when you're feisty, Blair."

A little thrill of excitement rolls up my spine, but I make myself ignore it. *I will not catch feelings for him. I will not catch feelings for the man who kidnapped me.*

Next thing I know, I'm in the kitchen, and Kylie is handing me a bowl, gesturing toward a pile of vegetables. "You can chop these."

Chop? I stare down at the vegetables with wide eyes as I pick up the knife carefully. Besides that one fall I thought a bob was a good idea, I've never chopped anything in my life.

"You good?" she asks when I just keep standing there, staring down at the vegetables.

"Yeah." I clear my throat. "Perfect." I blow out a breath and start my first attempt at cutting up vegetables—ever in my life. I'm slow as shit, I'm certain of that, but I'd prefer to keep the manicure I got last week intact as long as I can. Unless I want a squirrel to do my nails, there's not exactly a spa right up the street.

The cabin is quiet except for the small sounds of movement and water running and raw meat sizzling when Kylie dumps it into a pan.

And I can't deny it's a true contrast to my life in Boston. There's no marble or chandeliers or staff drifting through hallways.

There are just five people in one singular room—coexisting together.

I can't remember the last time my mom and dad and Bonnie and I were all in the same room together. The occasional dinner? Sure. But in the middle of the day? Hell no. Even growing up, my dad was always too busy with work, and my mom always had a million and one things on her social calendar to attend. Not to mention all the piano lessons and French lessons and whatever other thing Mom decided to sign Bonnie and me up for that kept us on the go all week long.

And yet I can't deny that there's something peaceful about having everyone in the same room together. It feels…calm and cozy. *It feels like how things used to be when Nanny Celeste was around.*

I push down memories of my childhood and refocus on slicing the vegetables, occasionally using more force than necessary.

But my eyes, they keep flitting toward the living room where Kane is adding blocks of wood to the fire, and his muscular forearms flex beneath his simple black T-shirt with each movement.

Heat flickers low in my stomach at the sight. *Stop it, Blair. Stop looking at him.*

I focus on the knife again.

This is adaptation. That's all this is. You're adjusting to survive.

Of course my body is going to seek the strongest person in the room. It's biology. It doesn't mean anything.

"Be careful," Kane whispers, and I look up to find him

standing right beside me. But when I follow his line of sight, I realize the knife is way too close to my fingers.

"Shit," I mutter and pull my hand back instinctively.

But Kane doesn't smirk, and he doesn't make a comment at my expense. Instead, he just steps behind me and wraps his arms around me to readjust my hands' position on the knife and cutting board.

"There ya go," he says. "Much safer."

That steadiness of his body calms my heart to a slow and efficient rhythm.

Goodness, why does this man have such an effect on me?

Rook walks into the kitchen and murmurs something to Kylie under his breath, and she laughs softly. He brushes his thumb across her cheek like it's the most natural thing in the world.

She doesn't look controlled.

She doesn't look owned.

She looks…connected to him. Like he's her prince and she's in a fairy tale. Like her entire world revolves around him. And frankly, he looks at her the exact same way.

Was she telling me the truth? Does she know more than I do? I mean, look at her. Look at how happy she looks right now…

I swallow and glance back at the cutting board.

You're romanticizing this, I argue with myself. *This is a cabin in the middle of nowhere with three blue-collar vampire men who apparently kidnap women in their free time.*

This is not supposed to be my destiny.

My destiny is New York. My destiny is the *blood of the three.* My destiny might've been Damien Snow.

My mom's voice is in my head, telling me how important

the bonding night is and how lucky I am and how special I am because of my bloodline. *Being chosen is an honor,* she's said more times than I can count. *Being chosen is your purpose.*

But then Kane's voice is in my ear, *Because you're not just something to me, Blair. You're fucking everything. And I don't want to own you. I just want you to want to be mine.*

My hand tightens around the knife, and my mind churns and burns with what has to be the equivalent of an existential crisis. *My parents wouldn't raise me my entire life for something monstrous…would they?*

No. Absolutely not. There's no way they would do that.

Instead of getting lost inside the minefield that is my own head, I focus on the rhythm of the room instead. There's no tension here. No one evaluating me or measuring my posture or tone. That absence feels strange. But more than that, it feels *right.*

I glance at Kane again when he isn't looking.

He's talking to Calloway about something mundane. *Supply runs. Gas mileage. Repairs.* His jaw is strong. His expression focused. There's no calculation in his eyes. No hunger.

When he looks at me, it's not like how Damien did at the mixer.

Damien's gaze lingered too long. It was clinical and assessing, and I didn't feel it in the pool of my belly.

But Kane's—

I look away before I finish that thought.

You're rewriting things. I try to bring myself back to reality. *This is what people do when they're disoriented. You imprint on the nearest constant. It doesn't mean he's right. It doesn't mean your entire life has been a lie. It just means you're adapting.*

"I'm just adapting," I murmur under my breath.

"What?" Kane asks from across the room.

"Nothing."

He watches me for a second longer than necessary.

And there it is again. That quiet steadiness.

I feel safest when he's near.

The realization is like stepping on glass, and I don't even know if it's true.

But you do know. You can feel it. You're drawn to him. And deep down, you believe him.

A sigh escapes my lungs. God, this is all so confusing.

But when I glance up and catch Kane watching me again, something inside me softens despite everything. He doesn't look victorious or possessive. He looks present, and those green eyes may as well be warmth personified.

He smiles, and I…smile back. And for one long second, I wonder what it would feel like to stop fighting whatever it is I feel whenever I'm around him.

God, I just need clarity.

I need to understand what is real and what isn't real.

I just need…*answers.*

17

KANE

BLAIR'S FIRST FULL DAY OF NOT BEING LOCKED IN my bedroom has gone smooth for the most part. She ate breakfast, helped Kylie make soup, and even ate said soup for dinner with Kylie.

Now, night is upon us, and the clouds rumble with a thunderstorm that's been threatening for the past hour.

Blair stands at the edge of the clearing with her arms folded tight across her chest. The wind lifts her hair and drops it again. The cabin light spills behind us in a soft rectangle, warm against the dark forest.

She hasn't looked at me once since we stepped outside, but after a long moment of silence, she turns to face me. Her expression isn't angry, but it's not exactly neutral either.

"Why did you kidnap me?" she asks. "I want to know the truth, Kane."

She is hanging by an emotional thread at the moment, and I know I have to choose my words carefully. I know that the truth of the situation—our reality—contradicts everything she's ever been told. If I have to keep answering the same questions over and over to help her believe, I'll do it.

"I have been telling you the truth. They were going to take you," I say finally. "New York wasn't what you thought it was."

"How in the hell could they take me if I was going willingly?" she retorts. "I packed my own bags, for fuck's sake."

"No," I say calmly. "You thought you were going willingly, but nothing can be willing, Blair, if all you're being told are lies. Damien Snow isn't who you think he is. None of the elites are. And what he invited you to is expressly forbidden by the Elite Council. If he touched you, used you, you'd have been ineligible for the auction altogether. And if he hadn't? You'd have been sold to the next vampire who would have treated you the exact same."

The wind shifts, carrying the scent of rain.

"I was raised around the elites," she snaps. "Pretty sure I know them better than you."

"You only know what they wanted you to know. You only saw what they wanted you to see."

She laughs, but it's brittle. "Well, I know I saw you kill two men in my driveway."

"Yeah. I did. Because their plans for you were worse," I answer without hesitation. "They'd have used and abused you before discarding you entirely. So, I preempted. Did to them before they could do to you. And I'd do it again."

Her breath stutters slightly at how easily I admit it. "You say that like it doesn't matter."

"It mattered."

"Then why aren't you acting like it?"

"Because if I hadn't killed them," I respond, "they would've delivered you to a man who sees you as property. He had zero good intentions, Blair. You weren't going to come back from New York, one way or another. Your mom and dad? Your sister Bonnie? All a fading memory of the past."

"Shut up." A little gasp escapes her throat. "You don't know that."

"But I do, Blair. I'm not lying to you. But everyone else has been."

Her composure cracks just a little. "My parents would never—"

"They raised you to believe being chosen is an honor because they probably think it is."

"Because it *is*," she retorts, but even I can feel her emotions waver over it. At this point, she's starting to question everything— including her parents.

"Is it, though?" I ask quietly. "Is it an honor to have men pay to own you? To treat you like property or a possession? To give you no choice when you're drawn from or your body used otherwise? Because that's how it would be, Blair. You, at their beck and call."

Her face goes pale. "That's not what it is."

"It's an auction, Blair. It's a fucking auction, and you were going to be sold to the highest bidder," I tell her the truth, even though I know it's impossibly hard for her to hear. "You think they're choosing wives? They're choosing bloodlines. It has absolutely nothing to do with love or romance or marriage. It has to do with the power your blood will bring them and because they want to breed you. That's all they want from you."

Her breathing gets faster. "You're lying."

"I wish I were."

"Do you even realize what you're saying right now?" She swallows hard. "You're basically telling me that my parents groomed me to believe a lie that ends with me being *trafficked*."

"I'm not saying they were grooming you intentionally, Blair. Honestly, I don't think they know the truth."

The first drop of rain hits our shoulders and then another and then another. We're both starting to get soaked, Blair's hair is already dripping wet, but she doesn't move.

So, I don't move either.

"Your parents think it's status," I say. "They probably even think they're providing you with a secure life, maybe accepting the dowry and squiring it away to maintain your lifestyle. But that's not the reality."

Her eyes shine with tears, and her bottom lip trembles.

But I have to keep going. I have to keep telling her the reality. "When was the last time any Windsor woman went to a Selection, Blair?"

"I don't know," she spits.

"You do know. But you don't want to think about the reality of it."

"Think about the reality of it?" she questions, and a deep exhale leaves her lungs. "Pretty sure my great-aunt Estelle is doing just fine in Rome. Because that's where she ended up with her vampire elite husband."

"So, you keep in touch with her?" I question, and she shakes her head.

"I don't want to talk about this anymore."

And there it is. The crack in her foundation. We both know

there's no one in the Windsor family who has had contact with Estelle Windsor since she was bought and sold to the elite in Rome at the ripe age of twenty-two. It's not information I should have, but I have it. Because I'll do anything I can to protect Blair. Even if she hates me for it.

Though, I can imagine her family has filled her head with all kinds of fantasies about what happened to her great-aunt. Hell, the elites have probably fed them the fucking lies. Those bastards probably let the Windsors believe Estelle lives this rich Italian life and simply doesn't have time to see or talk to anyone. She's too busy being wealthy and pampered and wonderful.

In reality, Estelle Windsor is dead. And she's been dead for a very long time. I almost open my mouth to tell her that, but I know it would be too much. I know it would be beyond cruel.

"Blair, I'm not trying to hurt you," I whisper. "In fact, hurting you feels akin to lighting myself on fire. It goes against everything inside me. I'm just trying to protect you. I'm just trying to keep you safe. That's it. That's all I'm doing."

Tears stream down her cheeks, and silence stretches between us.

And it takes everything inside me not to go to her and wrap her up in my arms. But I know she needs a moment. She needs space. And I refuse to bulldoze over that necessity.

Eventually, as the rain picks up, she takes one slow step toward me. "W-why?" she asks, but her voice is softer now. "Why do you feel like you need to protect me?"

Because you're mine. Because I am yours.

"You know why," I say quietly.

Her brows pull together. "No, I don't."

"You can feel it."

She just stands there, looking up at me while the rain runs down her temples and over her lashes. "I don't know what you're talking about."

"Yes, you do."

Her pulse jumps, and I move closer until there's barely any space between us.

"When I'm near you," I say, "your breathing changes."

She swallows.

"When I touch you, your body relaxes. When you're sleeping, your body seeks out mine."

Her fingers curl at her sides.

"When I pull away, your body tries to close the distance. Blair, you don't belong to anyone," I say quietly. "But you belong *with me.*"

Her eyes flash. "You don't get to decide who I belong with."

"*I would never decide for you.*"

She steps into me then, but it's not in anger. It's in frustration and confusion.

And then she kisses me.

There's no strategy in it. This isn't a test or manipulation. This is the bond. This is her trying to understand why she's so drawn to me. This is her not fighting against herself.

The kiss is slow and deep and not at all frantic like I'd expect. I can taste the salt of the rain on her lips, and when our tongues dance against each other, a small moan escapes her throat.

She slides her hands into my hair like she's trying to hold on to something solid, and I wrap my arms around her waist without thought.

The world narrows. The rain fades. And an arc of electricity flows from her chest and into mine.

I feel the exact second she stops resisting altogether. Her body softens, and her mouth doesn't hold back as she kisses me hard and deep and with every ounce of need and want and desire that flows inside her veins.

And I kiss her back. Because I can't not kiss her back. I can't not hold her body tight against mine. My cock grows hard as moans start to spill from her lips, and she presses her breasts against my chest.

When I finally pull back, she chases my mouth before she realizes I've stopped.

Her eyes open slowly.

"Why does it feel like this?" she whispers.

Because we're fated.

Because I would burn down the world to keep you safe.

Because I belong to you just as much as you belong to me.

"Because you're not fighting it right now," I say instead.

She tightens her fingers in my hair. "That's not it."

"I know."

She studies my face like she's looking for proof I'm lying. "You're telling me my whole life is a lie," she says quietly.

"I'm telling you it might not be what you think."

"And if you're wrong?"

"I'm a lot of things, Blair, but I'm not wrong. Not about this."

The rain intensifies. Her body presses closer again, and I wrap my arms around her and pull her tight against my chest.

She feels safe here with me. Not owned. Not controlled. Not trapped. *Safe.*

Her breath catches, and she pulls back like she's been burned. "This isn't real," she says.

"It's real, Blair."

Her eyes narrow. "Stop looking at me like that."

"Like what?"

"Like I'm yours."

You are. The truth sits heavy on my tongue, but I try to hold it back. I hold it back until I can't. "You are mine, Blair. You are mine, and I am yours."

"You can't know that," she whispers.

"I do. And so do you."

She stares at me like she's standing at the edge of something enormous. If she accepts it, everything changes. Her entire life, everything she was raised to believe, gets flipped on its head.

The rain soaks through her shirt, and she steps back slowly.

"You don't get to decide my destiny," she says.

"I'm not," I reply. "I just want you to see where she's trying to point you clearly."

She doesn't respond, but with tears streaming down her face, she turns and runs back toward the cabin. There's no anger or hatred or even fear pulsing through her veins. Just something dangerously close to recognition.

She doesn't have the term for it—*fated mates.*

But her body does.

And her heart does too.

18

I DON'T LOOK BACK AT HIM AS I RUN THROUGH the front door of the cabin.

If I look at him, I'll remember the way his mouth feels against mine. The way the world goes quiet whenever he pulls me close. The way my body softens whenever he's near.

I take the stairs too quickly. My wet shoes slip once on the wood, and I grab the railing to steady myself.

By the time I reach the bedroom, I'm shaking. But I don't know if it's from cold or panic or stress...*or the kiss.*

All I know is I feel out of control.

I close the door behind me and lean back against it. My reflection in the small mirror across the room looks unfamiliar. My clothes are drenched from the rain; my hair is plastered to my cheeks. My eyes are too bright. My lips are swollen.

I look *undone.*

I try to drag the soaked sweater over my head, but my fingers won't cooperate. The fabric tangles at my elbows, and my hands are trembling so hard I can't control them.

If he's telling the truth...

If Kylie's telling the truth…

Then everything I've been raised to believe…

My throat tightens, and I blink hard against the tears streaming from my eyes.

I yank at the sweater again, more frustrated than before, but it sticks to my skin, and my hands are worthless at doing even the simplest of tasks.

I don't hear him come in, but I *feel* the shift in the room. I feel the air change into something warmer, steadier, something that instantly makes my body want to turn around and run to him.

But I force my feet to stay frozen to the floor. Though, I do turn around. I do look at him.

Kane doesn't speak right away. He just takes in the sight of me standing there, soaked and shaking and half out of my clothes.

"Don't," I say, though I'm not sure what I'm asking.

He steps closer anyway, slow enough that I could put distance between us if I wanted to. "You're freezing," he says quietly.

"I'm fine."

"You're not."

His hands come up to the hem of the sweater still twisted around my arms. He pauses, giving me the space to pull back.

I don't.

He carefully lifts the fabric over my head, his gaze fixed somewhere above my shoulder instead of on me. The motion is efficient, almost clinical. There's no lingering touch of his fingers. No hungry look in his eyes.

Just a softness on his face. Just a tenderness in his touch.

The T-shirt I had on beneath the sweater is also drenched, and it sticks to my skin.

He reaches for it too, and this time, I hesitate for half a second before lifting my arms myself.

He peels the damp cotton away from my skin, eyes turned deliberately toward the wall. I feel the heat of him close to me, but he doesn't look at my exposed skin. He doesn't look at my bare stomach or breasts.

He grabs a towel from the bathroom and drapes it over my shoulders, and then he gently runs it down my arms to dry the rain from my skin. The gesture is unhurried, and his hands move across me with reverence.

My breathing slows without my meaning it to. Even my heartbeat calms down to a steady rhythm.

He kneels slightly to pull the soaked sweatpants from my legs, working carefully around my ankles. He never once lets his hands wander. Still never lets his eyes stray.

But it all feels more intimate than if he had.

He stands and reaches for one of his clean shirts. "Arms," he murmurs.

I lift them automatically.

He slides the shirt over my head and down my body, tugging it into place. His knuckles brush my collarbone for the briefest second before he steps back.

And without asking, he bends and scoops me up into his arms.

I don't protest. My body feels heavy suddenly, like the fight drained out of it all at once, and I melt into him. He carries me to the bed and lowers me onto the mattress. And I curl instinctively onto my side, facing the wall.

There's a small pause behind me.

Then the mattress dips.

His chest settles against my back, and he slides his arm around my waist. It's not tight or restraining; it's tender. It's solid. And his warm palm rests against my stomach.

"I've got you, Blair," he whispers.

Thunder rattles against the window, and the rain pelts the roof.

And Kane just holds me.

He doesn't press closer than necessary. He doesn't let his hands roam over my body. He just…*holds me,* in a way no one has ever held me before.

And the worst, most confusing part is how quickly my body responds.

My hands stop shaking. Tears stop streaming from my eyes. And the tightness in my chest loosens inch by inch.

I've been in houses with marble floors and ten-foot ceilings and security systems that could lock down an entire wing in seconds, but I have never felt as safe as I do right now, inside a wooden cabin wearing borrowed clothes.

I don't understand it.

I don't understand him.

But with Kane behind me and his arms cuddling my body to his chest, one truth slips past all the noise in my head before I fall asleep.

Whatever this is between us isn't stemming from weakness or manipulation or panic. It's something deeper. It's something I can't deny, no matter how hard I try.

19

KANE

LAIR ISN'T EXACTLY RUNNING STRAIGHT INTO my arms, but after last night, things feel a little less loaded today than they did yesterday. She came downstairs this morning freshly showered and smelling like the vanilla-scented body lotion I picked up for her the other day. She ate breakfast and didn't complain about the coffee tasting like "ass."

She even helped Kylie with the dishes.

All in all, she's finding her way here.

And trust me, I know what a feat that is for her. Blair might be spoiled and difficult and stubborn, but beneath the snobby exterior lies a woman who has had her entire world flipped upside down. She's soft and fragile and vulnerable, and I savor every single one of the moments she's let her guard down enough to just let me hold her.

Because, fuck, that's all I want to do.

It's nearing three in the afternoon, and she stands just inside the tree line surrounding the cabin.

Even while she's dressed in my flannel and sweatpants, she doesn't look like a woman who belongs in a place like this.

But she's trying. I know she's trying.

I can feel the sincerity through her intentions.

Though, she's also confused and still fighting against our bond. I can feel that too. It's like an incoming thunderstorm brewing, and you're not sure whether it's going to dump buckets of rain and lightning or pass over you without a drop of precipitation.

I walk across the lot in front of the cabin and head in her direction. She turns abruptly when she hears my boots crunch over gravel.

"You doing okay?"

At first, she says, "Yes," but that's quickly followed up by, "Actually, no."

"Anything I can do to help?"

"I need to call my mom." Her voice isn't sharp at all. If anything, it's pleading, and that's what breaks my heart the most. "She has to be worried sick about me, Kane," she continues when I don't immediately answer. "I wouldn't be surprised if they have a search party out for me at this point. My mom, my dad, my sister Bonnie, they're probably all losing their minds."

I don't tell her there's no search party. Or that her face isn't plastered across national news. I don't tell her because we still don't know why that's the case. And the last fucking thing I want to do is make her assume something that's not true—make her think her parents don't care about her.

"I know you want to call your mom. I get it. I really do, Blair. But—"

"No," she cuts me off. "No buts, Kane." She gestures vaguely at the forest. "I can't let them think I vanished. I can't let them think I've been, like, left for dead or something. Can you imagine how horrible it has to be for them right now? They are probably worried sick."

"I know." I sigh and run a hand through my hair. "You're right."

"So, you'll let me call her?"

My chest aches over what my answer has to be. "No. I'm sorry, but no."

"You don't get to say no," she says quietly, but I can already see the sheen of tears behind her eyes. I can hear the shake in her voice.

"If you call them right now," I explain, "you tell them where you are. Or you tell them enough that someone tracks it. Then this place isn't safe anymore. Not just for you or for me, but all of us. For Kylie. For Rook. For Cal. I can't put them in a bad situation they didn't ask for." I've sure as shit already done enough by bringing her here against her will.

"Seriously, Kane?" She laughs, and it sounds almost hysterical. "You think my parents are going to send someone here? You think they're dangerous?"

I don't answer fast enough, and a small gasp escapes her lungs. "You do. You think my parents are dangerous."

"No." I choose my words carefully. "I think they're involved with people who are."

"My father is not some criminal mastermind," she snaps. "He sits on boards. He donates to hospitals."

"And he walks inside elite vampire circles."

She stiffens. "That's different."

"It isn't, Blair."

She shakes her head, stepping back like I physically pushed her. "You don't know anything about my family."

"I know enough."

"Enough to what?" she fires back. "To decide I'm better off cut off from them? To decide I don't get to hear my mother's voice ever again?"

The word mother cracks on the way out because it's the real wound. Her mom is at the surface of all her current turmoil.

"She raised me," Blair continues, her voice trembling. "She prepared me my whole life. You don't get to step in for mere days and act like you know better than the woman who birthed me. Sure, she wasn't always the greatest at times, but what parent is? She's consistent and only wants the best for me. That's all she's ever wanted. For me to have the best of everything."

I keep my mouth shut. Mostly because I don't know what to say. I don't think I know Blair's mother better than she knows her, but I know more about the elites than she does. She's been told lie after lie, and the fairy-tale façade she has in her head doesn't even come close to the reality.

Does her mother know the truth? I honestly don't fucking know.

When I don't say anything, my silence triggers her even more. Her eyes widen, filling with something raw. "You think my mother would hand me to monsters," she says, and it's not a question.

"I didn't say that." I run a hand through my hair. "I think she believes she's doing what's best."

"That's not an answer."

"It's the only one I've got."

Her breathing turns ragged. "You won't let me call them," she says, more to herself than to me.

"I will, eventually, but not yet."

"When?" she demands.

"When I know it won't get you hurt."

"You don't get to decide that!" she shouts.

My connection to her sparks inside me. *You're mine. Not property. Not ownership. But mine in the way the ocean belongs to the moon. I can't let anything happen to you. It would kill me.*

I want to tell her the truth—tell her she's my fated mate. Tell her she's my destiny. Tell her the universe created us to be together—to be one. But she already has too much on her plate right now, and I fear that would simply push her over the edge.

"If you call them," I say quietly, "you risk walking straight back into the same hands I pulled you from. Or worse, bringing them straight to our door. And I refuse to put my brothers and Kylie in that situation."

"That won't happen, Kane. I'll make sure of it."

"You can't make sure of that, Blair. It will be out of your control."

"You killed two men in my driveway!" she screams. "You dragged me into the woods! And now you're telling me my parents can't be trusted?"

Her pulse spikes, and I can see it thrumming at her neck. I can hear it rushing through her veins. And I see a million different emotions flit across her face and a million more intentions roll through her head. Her mind is so all over the place that I can't even pinpoint what she intends to do.

"Why are you doing this to me?" she asks, and tears stream down her cheeks.

Because I love you. Because it feels like you're my whole fucking world. "Because I have to, Blair. Because I fucking have to."

She takes a step backward.

Then another.

"Blair," I warn, but I don't command.

She shakes her head violently. "I just need a minute, Kane," she says, voice breaking. "I just need a fucking minute."

Her intent shifts, and it isn't escape or betrayal. It's *resolve.*

And then, she turns and walks straight into the trees.

I move instantly, but then I hesitate because she's asking for a minute, and her intentions aren't showing me anything that would give me the power to stop her. She's merely trying to understand it all. And understanding it all, truly wrapping her head around the truth, comes with an emotional toll of grief and anger and rage and sadness. Deep, deep sadness.

So, I give her a few moments of space.

By the time I surge forward into the forest, she's already deeper than she should be.

"Blair!" I call once.

She doesn't answer, but my body can sense her heavy breaths and fast heartbeat.

She's running now.

Fuck. I have to stop her before she does something reckless.

I have to stop her before *they* get to her first.

20

I DON'T KNOW HOW LONG I RUN.

But I know the forest doesn't give a shit about me. It doesn't part or soften; it just keeps existing in a thick and endless green that feels almost violent every time it smacks me in the face.

My lungs burn. My legs shake. But I don't stop.

Because if I stop, he'll track me down. I know Kane will. That's the advantage of being a vampire. They're faster and stronger than us humans. They can track your scent and hear you breathing from miles away.

But I've been prepared for this moment my entire life. Well, not the running in the stupid forest part, but the fact that I know the things that make it hard for vampires to track you. Being raised in a family that's close with the elite, I've learned plenty while eavesdropping during parties my parents threw at our mansion.

I also was a voracious reader as a little girl—wanting to learn and understand everything I possibly could about what my future vampire husband would be like.

I hop across a muddy creek bed and make a point to remove

the flannel shirt from my body and toss it on the ground. I'm only in sweatpants and one of Kane's white T-shirts at this point, but I don't care. I zigzag run in the opposite direction of the shirt and just keep moving as fast as my legs can take me.

I'm a mess, but I don't care.

I just need to get somewhere that I can use a phone so I can call my mom.

I don't know what I'm going to do once I call her, but I just need to talk to her. That's the only thought that feels solid. *If I can just talk to her. If I can just get answers, I'll feel better.*

I think I'll feel better.

I *hope* I'll feel better.

The ground dips suddenly, and I stumble straight into another creek bed that's filled with freezing water. A sharp gasp rips out of me as my shoe sinks into the mud, and I catch myself on a slick rock and nearly fall.

Shit!

By the skin of my teeth, I manage to catch myself before I launch my entire body into the muddy water. Though, nearly half of me is already drenched.

Goodness, it's so cold. My teeth start chattering and my muscles want to shiver, but I just keep running. I scramble up the opposite bank and continue moving.

My hair sticks to my face and my borrowed clothes cling damp against my skin, and I know there's no way I look anything like myself.

Right now, I probably don't look like Blair Windsor at all.

My mother would be horrified to see me like this.

The trees thin without warning, and sunlight starts to hit my face until the forest ends abruptly.

My eyes catch sight of pavement—a narrow two-lane road cutting through nothing.

Oh my God! Thank everything!

My lungs scream and my muscles ache, but I don't stop running until I'm right at the edge of the road. I stand there for a second, swaying slightly, trying to decide if this is real. And I keep glancing over my shoulder, expecting to see Kane's face appear.

But he doesn't come.

Did he not even try to track me?

I frown, but I also look out toward the road again. Instantly, I spot a small maroon sedan heading my way. It's a horrible color for a car, but right now, it's the best-looking car I've ever seen in my life.

And I know it's completely reckless, but I step forward and start waving both of my hands in the air to get their attention.

The car slows, and before they come to a stop, I see it's an older couple inside. A man and a woman with kind faces and curious eyes.

Okay, this is probably fine. They don't look murder-y or anything.

The window rolls down.

"Oh my goodness, dear," the woman says softly as she takes in my disheveled appearance. "Are you all right?"

"Yes." The lie comes easily. "I just got a little turned around hiking, and I'm hoping maybe you can give me a ride into town?"

I have no idea what town we're near, but I'm hoping they know.

The man studies me for a long second, but then he unlocks the door.

"Of course. Hop in."

Relief floods so fast it almost makes me dizzy, and I scramble into the back seat. The car smells like peppermint gum and clean upholstery.

"Here you go, sweetheart." The woman hands me tissues over her shoulder, and I wipe at my face, trying to feel like myself again.

"What is the closest town?" I ask.

"Ashford Hollow," the man replies. "About fifteen minutes."

"And what state is Ashford Hollow in?"

"Connecticut, dear." The woman glances over her shoulder to meet my eyes, her mind clearly growing confused on why I don't even know what the hell state I'm in.

"Okay, phew. I was praying I didn't hike myself to Massachusetts or something crazy."

They both laugh.

"Do either of you happen to have a phone I can borrow?"

The phone is warm in my hands when the woman passes it back to me, but when I look down at the screen, I can see there's no signal.

"There's no service out here," she updates. "But once we get into town, you should be able to make a call."

I nod and stare out the window, and my mind races with a million different things.

Kane. The way he looked hurt instead of angry when I walked into the forest.

The way he makes me feel. And the way my body feels like it's aching for him the more distance I put between us.

The way I miss him already. Really, really miss him.

I've never felt so confused in my entire life, and I force it all out of my head and try to focus.

I just need to get into town and call my mom.

She'll have the answers I need.

21

KANE

ER SCENT TEARS THROUGH THE AIR—SHARP with salt and adrenaline and heartbreak. She isn't thinking clearly, I know that much. And her intentions are so fucking jumbled right now, so unpredictable, I can't even read them.

All I know is she's running.

I spot a creek bed and my flannel shirt buried in the mud.

"Blair!" I call out for her.

I move farther into the forest, trying to follow her scent, but it fractures when I reach another small creek bed. The gravel is disturbed, and I can see an imprint of her shoe in the mud.

But still, she's nowhere to be found.

Fuck!

It takes me a moment to catch her scent again, but when I do, I pick up my pace, sprinting as hard and fast as I can. And I don't stop running until I'm out of the forest and my boots hit pavement.

Her scent is strong here. *Fear. Exhaustion. Damp cotton.*

But so is the smell of gasoline and rubber and other humans.

I crouch down and press my hand briefly to the asphalt of

the road and feel the warmth of fresh tires. Instantly, I know she didn't keep running. She caught a ride.

Fuck!

"I fucked up," I say loud enough in hopes that my brother Cal's super ears will hear.

Not even ten seconds later, inside my head, Rook's voice cuts through. *What's going on?*

Blair's gone, I answer back through my thoughts. *She ran. Through the forest. Hit the road. Hitched a ride.*

Fuck. Where are you? Rook questions.

Rural road east of the cabin, my mind responds. *Pretty sure she's heading toward Ashford Hollow.*

I straighten and turn toward the direction of the nearest town. It's the only place within a reasonable distance. If she got picked up, that has to be where they're headed.

I move along the tree line instead of the road. I run as fast as I fucking can but still controlled enough not to draw attention. Halfway there, her scent strengthens briefly.

Then fades.

Then strengthens again.

Vehicle. Windows down. Older humans.

I can almost reconstruct the current scene in my head.

Fuck. The only reason I'm in this fucking situation is because I hesitated when she first walked into the forest, determined to give her space.

Cal's coming to help, Rook tells me.

I keep running. My chest throbs with discomfort of her being so far away from me, of her unknowingly putting herself at risk like this.

And I silently hope I can get to her before something terrible happens.

I should've stopped her. I should've remembered that we're not just lovers—we're mates. And that means everything is exponentially worse when we're apart.

22

A GIANT SIGN WITH A BIG SMILING SUN THAT reads, **WELCOME TO ASHFORD HOLLOW! WHERE EVERYONE IS A FRIEND!** confirms my hitchhiking ride-givers as truthful, and my shoulders fall an inch farther away from my ears.

I've never set foot in a small town, but from what I've seen in reruns of *Gilmore Girls,* this is the epitome of one. We go through one singular streetlight before moving past a gas station and a diner that has two pickup trucks parked outside.

This place feels small. Too small, if I'm being honest.

The nice man named Todd pulls into a parking lot that sits in front of what has to be the world's tiniest grocery store—Ashford Hollow Market.

"Sweetheart, Todd is going to park right here, and you can try to use my cell phone again, okay?" the woman in the passenger seat updates.

"Thank you," I say, but my voice feels so freaking tiny and unfamiliar. Every cell inside my body is screaming for me to get out of the car and, I don't know, head in the direction I just came from. Which is nuts.

Is he looking for me? Did he chase after me? Is he worried about me? Are not the thoughts a woman like me should be having about her blue-collar kidnapper.

The woman—whose name I can't remember, even though she told it to me—turns around to face me and nods down at the screen of her phone that's still in my hands. "Looks like you've got four bars, so you should be able to get service now."

I stare down at the screen, focusing intently on trying to remember phone numbers. This is where technology screws us all. I'm so used to just finding the name and hitting call that it's hard to remember the digits to my parents' phones.

I shut my eyes and try to envision my mom's contact information, and thankfully, it only takes me a few seconds to put it together.

Phone to my ear, I hear it start ringing.

Once. Twice. Three times.

Then it rolls over to voice mail.

Shit. My stomach drops to my damn toes.

I hang up and work to remember my dad's number. This one comes easier. Phone to my ear again, I shut my eyes tight and pray he answers.

"Dammit," I mutter when I get his voice mail too.

I hang up and try both of their numbers again. And when I still have no success, dread forms a deep pit in my stomach.

"They didn't pick up?" the woman asks.

I shake my head.

"Well, Todd and I are going to run into the grocery store

really quick, but you can wait here and keep trying with my phone while we're inside, okay?"

I nod. "Thanks. I appreciate it."

They get out of the car, and I sit there trying to understand what in the hell is happening right now. A normal, sane person would have told this couple that she has been kidnapped and to take her to the nearest police station. But that's not what I did at all.

Because you believe Kane. And Kylie. And Kane's brothers.

I try to call my mom and dad *again*, but neither of them answers.

I'm tempted to demon dial or text 9-1-1 over and over until they see it, but something holds me back from going that far. I don't know what I'm afraid it will create. Panic? Fear? A swarm of police showing up right here in this parking lot? *Putting Kane and Kylie and Rook and Cal in danger?*

The old Blair would've done that in a heartbeat.

But current Blair? The one who's left after being kidnapped? The one who knows what it feels like to kiss Kane and to sleep in his bed? The one who survived using three-in-one body wash and helped Kylie make soup and didn't perish from not being able to do her twenty-step nightly skin care routine? She's changed.

I stare out toward the one streetlight, and the wind cuts through the damp fabric of Kane's borrowed shirt. I wrap my arms around myself and step away from the car, already dialing my mother's number again.

When she doesn't answer, I press my palm to my forehead, trying to think.

There's only one other person who would know the reality

of everything. Only one other person who probably knows why I went missing in the first place. *Holland.*

My mind fills with memories of Kylie warning me about him. But the part that's desperate to see my family overrules it all. *Surely my parents have been in contact with him. Surely he's probably a part of the search party too.*

I shut my eyes and lean my head back and try like hell to remember his phone number.

It takes me three whole attempts and having to talk to two random strangers who are most definitely not Holland Thorne before I can figure out his actual number.

He answers on the first ring. "Hello?"

"Holland, it's Blair. Blair Windsor," I say, and I hate how small my voice sounds.

"Blair?" he questions, but his tone isn't surprised. It's just steady in a way that makes me furrow my brow.

"Yeah. I…it's me," I say, and I hesitate over what I should even tell him about my situation. I don't know if he knows who kidnapped me from my driveway or killed the two men who came to pick me up. *And you don't want him to know if he doesn't already.*

"Are you okay?"

It's a real mindfuck when you find yourself covering for your kidnapper, but that is my situation.

Because no matter what you're trying to tell yourself, you're in love with Kane.

The thoughts steal my breath.

"Blair? You still there?"

"Y-yeah," I say, swallowing against the tightness in my throat. "I'm okay. I'm good. I…I don't have my phone, and I need to get in touch with my parents but they're not answering. It's probably because they think it's a spam call or something. I had to borrow someone's phone."

"Where are you, Blair?"

"Uh…" I pause, unsure if I should tell him, but end up telling him anyway. "It's this little rural town. Ashford Hollow."

"I'm nearby," he says immediately. "Stay where you are."

Nearby? Why would he be nearby?

And I almost ask him exactly that, but then he adds, "I'll take you to your parents. They're waiting in New York."

"What? Why are my parents in New York?"

"Just sit tight, Blair. I'll be there in a few, and I'll explain everything to you. Just glad that you're okay. Just glad that you're safe."

Relief already starts to seep in. Clearly, he knows what's happening. He's been in touch with my parents. And soon, they'll know that I'm okay. Soon, I'll be able to talk to my mom and get some answers. Some clarity.

Before Todd and his wife come out of the grocery store, a black Escalade pulls into the lot and Holland steps out. He's wearing a suit and is perfectly composed in all the ways I'm used to men in my life being.

He's not urgent or frantic but completely calm. I should probably find comfort in that, but something makes me feel a little on edge.

"You good?" he asks, smiling softly in my direction.

I nod, and when I turn back toward the couple's car, I spot them walking out of the grocery store with a few bags in their hands. When they close the distance between us, I hand the nice lady her phone. "I really appreciated your help today."

She looks toward where Holland stands by his Escalade.

"Is that your ride, sweetheart?"

"Yes. Thanks again for everything."

"Of course, of course," she says and reaches out to give me a tight hug. "You take care of yourself, okay?"

"I will."

And then I walk toward where Holland has the back passenger door held open for me.

Once I'm inside and buckled in, he hops in the driver's seat and starts heading out of the parking lot. But I can't stop myself from looking back. At Todd and his friendly wife. At the small downtown area. At the forest.

Waiting for Kane's face to appear.

But it doesn't.

"It should only take us two hours to get to New York," Holland updates.

"Did you tell my parents you were picking me up?"

"Of course," he says. "And Damien knows you're safe too."

Damien? What does Damien have to do with this? I don't want to see him.

"I really just want to see my mom and dad," I tell him, and he just smiles at me in the rearview mirror.

"Everything is going to be okay, Blair. You're safe."

But his words don't match how I'm feeling inside. I don't feel safe. I feel…uncertain. I feel…on edge. I feel unsteady.

"Here, have a drink of water," he says and hands me a bottle from the front seat. "I also have some snacks too."

"I'm not hungry."

"At least drink the water, Blair."

I let out a deep sigh, but I comply with his request. I mean, considering I just ran through the forest for God knows how long, I am thirsty. I'm probably hungry too, but the idea of food right now is repulsive.

I take a sip from the bottle and then a few more sips, and before I know it, I've chugged the whole damn thing.

Holland keeps his eyes on the road the entire time, but everything else about him feels like it's focused on me.

Why was he nearby when I called?

Why hasn't he asked me anything about what happened?

Why hasn't he mentioned anything about my mom and dad being worried or a search party or...?

My thoughts come to an abrupt halt when my eyes grow heavy and my mind turns foggy. My stomach clenches with nausea, and all of a sudden, the back seat feels like it's spinning.

I feel...strange.

I feel...

"Holland? I don't...feeeeel...so...goooood," I say, but my words come out like I'm talking in slow motion.

"Just rest your eyes, Blair. Everything will be fine."

I try to open my mouth to say something, but then everything goes black.

Trust is a funny thing—sometimes, you fight it, even though your whole body agrees. And sometimes, you accidentally give it to the entirely wrong person for free.

23

I HIT THE OUTSKIRTS OF ASHFORD HOLLOW AT full speed. This a tiny fucking town that we've occasionally used on supply runs when we're at the cabin. It's located in Connecticut and only about two hours from New York City.

As I break through the tree line, my eyes catch sight of an Escalade pulling out of the parking lot of the only grocery store in town.

It's blacked-out, tinted windows, and polished in the way that screams money.

She's in there. I can feel it with every cell in my body.

Fuck.

For half a second, I consider crossing the asphalt in a blur, ripping open the door, and dragging her out before anyone can blink.

But there are witnesses everywhere—local humans just milling about, doing their daily business of going to the grocery store and diner and bakery that sits at the end of the small downtown area. Security cameras are mounted above the shops. A police station is across the street.

There are too many fucking eyes.

The SUV turns toward the interstate, her scent trailing behind it, and I just stand there, with dread overcoming my senses.

"She's in there."

The voice is calm, coming out of nowhere, but I instantly know it's my brother. I turn to find Cal standing there, clearly having hauled some serious ass to catch up with me.

I don't answer. I'm already watching the angle of the turn, the direction of the sun on the windshield, calculating distance and speed.

The Escalade merges onto the highway ramp.

"I can't fucking tell who is driving it."

"Holland," Cal says, and instantly, my skin crawls.

Holland is a fucking shield. And unfortunately, that means he's capable of completely blocking me out. Even Rook wouldn't be able to tap into his fucking head. But Cal can hear anything he says out loud.

"Fuck!" I should've never let her out of my fucking sight. I shouldn't have given her space. I shouldn't have cared if she would've hated me for it. I shouldn't have cared about anything but protecting her.

"Take a breath, brother," Cal says, his eyes shut as he focuses intently. "He's on the phone right now."

All I can do is wait—hoping and fucking praying Cal can hear something that gives us an idea of where in the fuck he's taking her.

"They cleaned the driveway," Cal says finally. "The two guys you killed. They were removed before her parents saw anything. Her parents think she made the flight. They think she's with

Damien Snow." He goes still again, listening deeper. "Holland just said that Blair thinks she's going to see them."

My jaw tightens. Now it's making more sense why we've yet to hear any reports of Blair Windsor going missing. Every time Cal has left the cabin for surveillance, he never saw any action at the Windsor mansion. No police cars. No private investigators. No missing persons reports.

And you'd think with a family like the Windsors, her disappearance would've been on every major news source in the country.

But the elites made damn sure Blair's parents were kept in the dark, all the while Blair believed her family has been worried sick searching for her.

As far as her parents know, she's in New York. With Damien Snow. Exactly where she's supposed to be.

The SUV is almost out of sight now, swallowed by highway traffic.

"He's talking about us. The Elite Council knows you're the one who took her," Cal updates. "They know Rook took Kylie. They're offering a million dollars for each of our heads to any gofer who can track us down."

That should put me on edge, but I don't give a shit about any of it right now. "What about Blair?"

"He's taking her to New York. To Damien." Cal's expression hardens. "They have plans…"

My jaw ticks. "What plans?"

Cal doesn't answer right away, and I get up in his face. "What fucking plans, Cal?"

"They plan to use whatever means possible to get information out of her. About us. About you," Cal says, and his voice comes out so ragged I know there's more he's not saying—I imagine it has a lot to do with what happens when she's no longer an asset. "And she's out."

"Out? What does that mean?"

"He gave her something," Cal says, his eyes searching mine in concern. "He gave her something to knock her out."

He. Drugged. Her.

He fucking drugged her!

My chest constricts brutally, and rage flows through my body like a tidal wave. But the fury doesn't explode. It condenses. It settles. It sharpens like a fucking knife.

I turn toward the highway. "I'm going to New York."

Cal doesn't argue because he knows I don't have a choice. He knows I will do anything to save her. And he knows that my next move involves killing whoever the fuck stands in my way.

I step forward, already calculating routes, distance, entry points.

They have no idea what they just set in motion.

I'm either leaving New York with Blair, or I'll die trying. But if it's the second, I won't do it without killing every single motherfucker I can before I go.

24

ARBLE IS THE FIRST THING I SEE WHEN I open my eyes, a contrast to a room full of wood in every way.

White marble floors, floor-to-ceiling windows, and expensive works of art hanging on the wall. There's even an ornate fireplace sitting directly across from me.

The entire wall to my right is completely glass, showcasing a breathtaking city view of skyscrapers.

I'm in New York.

I've been to this city too many times not to recognize it instantly.

My head throbs and my mouth is dry, and there's a strange metallic taste in the back of my throat. I work to push myself up to a sitting position. I'm in a cushy king-sized bed, surrounded by a soft, fluffy gold comforter and too many pillows to count.

Where am I?

The last thing I remember is sitting in Holland's Escalade. He handed me some water to drink, and then everything just went black.

Did I fall asleep?

I swing my legs off the bed, and my eyes continue to take inventory of the room. It's large and pristine with modern art and glass tables and an impressive chandelier hanging from the ceiling.

Everything is curated and expensive, and it looks exactly like what I've been raised around my entire life. It's the opposite of the cabin. And nothing like Kane's simple bedroom.

And it feels incredibly unsafe.

"Hello?" I call out. "Holland? Mom? Dad?"

My voice sounds tiny in the open space.

But it doesn't take long before the door opens, and Damien Snow walks in. He's wearing a perfect suit, his body showcased with perfect posture, and a perfectly controlled smile on his lips. He's exactly as I expected he'd be—and somehow as opposite of perfect as opposite can be.

"Hello, Blair," he greets.

"How did I get here?" I question. "I know Holland picked me up, but I don't remember anything after that."

"You fell asleep. He carried you in."

My eyes go wide. "He carried me in?"

Damien nods, but I don't miss the way his eyes narrow as he looks me up and down. "You need to take a shower. Get in some fresh clothes. I have everything you need."

I glance down and quickly realize I'm still covered in dry mud. I'm still wearing Kane's T-shirt and sweatpants. But I don't give a shit about my clothes or a shower right now.

"Where are my parents?" I ask. "Holland said they were in New York. Are they staying here with you?"

"They're fine," he says smoothly. "They went back to Boston."

I jerk my head back. "What?"

"They didn't need to stay," he replies. "Everything was handled."

Handled? My head pulses harder.

"Where is Holland?"

"He left."

I glance around the room again. The marble. The skyline. The art. It's everything I've always known. Everything that's supposed to mean stability.

And yet, all I feel right now is fear.

"I need to call my mother," I say.

"No."

I stare at him. "What do you mean, no?"

"You don't need to."

He steps closer to me, his movements slow and controlled. "It's time for you to take a shower, Blair." And once his knees bump the edge of the mattress, he reaches out to run his fingers through my hair.

My body recoils before I can stop it.

His eyes narrow slightly, but a faint smile touches his mouth.

"Yeah," he murmurs. "You were worth the trouble."

Trouble? My pulse spikes, and fear blossoms in my stomach.

"You'll be valuable," he adds.

Valuable? The word echoes in my head, and something cold spreads through my chest.

"Uh… I need to leave, Damien. I really need to talk to my parents. I think we should probably reschedule this trip," I say, but his answer comes without hesitation.

"No, you don't need to leave because you belong here. With

me. We have lots of things to do together, Blair." His smile makes my skin crawl. "And I'm sure you have lots of things to tell me, about where you've been and who you've been with the past few days."

"I really need to go," I say and rise to my feet. I move past him to walk toward the door, but when my fingers wrap around the handle, it doesn't budge.

And not even a second later, he's behind me and his hand clamps around my arm.

"Don't."

"Let go of me." I twist, but he simply picks me up as if I weigh nothing, carries me back over to the bed, and drops me down unceremoniously. The shock of it all knocks the air from my lungs.

"You're here now," he says, adjusting his cuff like nothing just happened. "I paid good money for you."

The words slam into me. *Paid. Good. Money.*

"Maybe too much," he continues coolly. "Considering the trouble you've caused."

Everything inside me starts to shake, and Kane's voice flashes through my mind. All the things he told me. All the things he warned me about.

"I need to go home," I say, swallowing against the ball of emotion in my throat. "I need to talk to my mom."

He looks at me like I'm naïve. "You don't need to do anything right now besides take a shower and wash the vile stench of *him* off your skin."

Him. He means Kane. I know without a doubt.

"The bathroom is behind that door." He points across the room. "Everything you need is in there and in the large closet near the fireplace. I'll be back when you've finished, and then we can start the process of checking if you're still intact."

"Intact?"

"Your virginity. You smell like you're still a virgin, but I want to be sure."

The urge to vomit overwhelms me.

Oh my God. Oh my God. I should've never left the cabin. I should've never fucking left the cabin!

Without another word, he walks to the door, doing something briefly on his phone, before it unclicks and opens.

He steps into the hallway. The door closes behind him, and the lock clicks firmly in place.

And I sprint into the bathroom and throw up.

I fear that I might not leave this place alive.

25

KANE

Manhattan doesn't sleep. The city hums—engines, voices, footsteps, a thousand overlapping intentions bleeding into the air. Greed. Impatience. Hunger. Desire.

Normally, I can ignore it.

But right now, it presses against my skull like a hammer.

Cal leans against the brick wall of the small alley we're standing inside. His eyes are half closed, and he's focusing hard, trying to let his ears pick up anything he can. Across the street, the fancy skyscraper rises sixty stories high. It's the kind of place filled with residential penthouses that are built for men who believe money makes them untouchable.

And Damien Snow lives at the very top.

Cal tilts his head slightly, and I can only imagine what a fucking maze it is filtering through all this noise to identify conversations that will help us get to Blair.

"Front desk rotates every twenty minutes," he murmurs. "Two guards in the private lobby. Keycard elevators only."

I keep my eyes on the tower.

"Service routes?" I ask.

"There's a loading dock on the west side," he says. "Maintenance elevator. No cameras inside the shaft."

I nod once.

"Damien's penthouse has two guards outside his door," Cal adds after another moment.

All of it's good info to have when I'm planning on barreling through that slimefuck's place like the Kool-Aid man, but the words barely register because something else hits me hard.

It's fear, but it doesn't stem from confusion or anger. It stems from clarity, and behind it sits outright terror and the desperate need to escape.

Blair.

The closer I am to her, the more I can feel her. The more I can sense her intentions and her emotions and every beat of her heart. Her pulse is racing. Her breaths are short and choppy. She's not just scared; she's terrified.

Real, visceral panic rips through my chest like a blade.

"I need to get to her now. Right fucking now."

Cal looks at me.

"I can feel her, man. She's scared shitless. She wants to escape. And her intentions aren't from naïveté. They're from pure fucking realization of the truth." I meet his eyes. "Do you know enough to get us inside?"

"Well, I can never be certain. But I don't think we have time for certainty, do we?"

I shake my head and swallow hard against the urge to burn this whole fucking city to the ground just to get to her.

The distance between us feels unbearable.

And her fear is making it impossible for me to temper my rage.

"Is it safe to say this little road trip is going to end with a body count?" Cal questions, and I don't hesitate to respond.

"Yep."

There's no turning back now.

I'm going in.

26

BLAIR

I STILL HAVEN'T SHOWERED. I STILL HAVEN'T changed my clothes. I haven't done anything but pace this room that Damien has locked me inside without any destination but outright panic in mind.

I fucked up. I know I fucked up.

I should've never left the cabin.

I should've listened to Kane.

I should've believed him.

I know that now with absolute certainty. *But what good does it do me now, huh?*

Tears prick my eyes, and I walk into the bathroom to look at my reflection in the mirror. I'm a mess in every sense of the word. My hair is a tangled mess down my shoulders. My eyes are bloodshot red from my crying jags. And the only makeup on my face is dried mud from the creek bed I fell in.

My mother would be horrified.

I lift the hem of Kane's muddied white T-shirt and bury my face into the material, drowning all of my senses in the faint scent of him. More tears spill from my lids, and my entire body aches with the realization that I'll probably never see him again.

I'll never get to feel his lips on mine or his arms wrapped around me.

I'll never get to look into his green eyes and watch them shift violet in the light.

I'll never get to tell him that I love him. That I'm done fighting whatever this is between us. That I'm his.

And God, what a devastating realization that is.

Tears flow down my cheeks and into his shirt, and I just let them because I can't control them. Because I can't control the surge of emotion I feel at the mere idea of never seeing him again.

I step out of the bathroom, dragging in a shaky breath. When I peer inside the closet near the fireplace, desperate to keep moving with the sole purpose of survival, that's when I see it—*my suitcase*. The one I packed in preparation for my big, fancy, hope-filled trip to New York.

God, that feels like a million years ago.

I was a different girl back then. A completely different Blair.

I don't know why Damien has it, but it doesn't matter. I can only think of one thing. I drop to my knees and yank it open. My hands move frantically, rooting through clothes, shoes, makeup—none of it registers—until I find my doll.

My vampire with the green-violet eyes and pale hair and Kane's perfect smile.

A broken sound escapes me as I clutch it to my chest, squeezing my eyes shut while tears spill down my cheeks. I glance back into the suitcase—at all the expensive things I used to think I needed.

None of them are priorities anymore.

I just need Kane.

But I've ruined any chance of that ever happening again.

27

KANE

CAL LAID OUT A PLAN THAT FEELS AS IF IT WILL create the least amount of disruption and attention. At least, I fucking hope that's the case. At this point, he's the only logical one out of the two of us. I'm hanging by a thread with my fated mate locked in some fucking bloodthirsty lunatic's penthouse.

I swear on everything, if he fucking touches her, I will murder him.

"Relax," Cal whispers. "You gotta rein it in, brother. Save the rage for when we're in his place."

He's not wrong to chastise me. The goal right now is to avoid as many security guards and people as we can. The goal is to get to the sixtieth floor with zero witnesses or confrontations.

We move around the block toward the loading dock on quick feet. The alley behind the tower is quiet. Empty delivery trucks sit by a bay that's lined with dumpsters, and a steel door secures the back entrance.

Cal listens again.

"I'm only hearing three men inside. Pretty sure it's a combination of maintenance staff and a security guard," he updates.

I reach for the handle on the steel door, and it opens without issue. We slip inside and start the quiet trek down a concrete corridor that's lined with fluorescent lights that buzz above our heads.

Footsteps approach before we've taken ten steps, and both Cal and I sneak into a utility closet. The footsteps pass us by, two men laughing and chatting about something innocuous, and then they disappear out the same door we entered.

"We're clear," Cal says, and we head out of the utility closet and finish walking the rest of the way down the corridor.

But just as we round the corner, heading for the staff elevator, we come face-to-face with a man dressed in all black. He's looking down at his phone but still walking toward us.

"Vamp," Cal whispers.

"Gofer," I add.

Being raised in a world where we're constantly surrounded by the elites' fucking gofers, it's really easy to spot them in the wild. We've been to school with these fucks. Played hockey against them in our Concordia rec league.

He looks up from his phone, and his gaze meets mine for a brief, shocked moment before he looks at Cal.

"Slater brothers," he spits, and I feel his intention spike— *gun, kill.*

Of course he's got a gun. The elites and their fucking gofers never play fair. Not in life. Not in battle. Not in love. Not in any-fucking-thing.

I move before he can draw. My hand closes around his throat, and by the time he reaches for the gun, Cal has already ripped it free from his holster and thrown it across the room.

Crack, I snap his neck with quick but brutal force.

His body goes limp in my hold, and I slowly lower him to the floor. Cal grabs his feet, and we scoot the dead bastard across the tile floor and discard him in a closet near the maintenance lift.

"Shit just got real," Cal mutters as I tap the button for the elevator.

"Pretty sure shit got real the morning Rook kidnapped Kylie."

Cal chuckles softly. "Yeah."

The elevator doors slide open, and we step inside. Cal hits the number sixty on the wall, and the doors slide closed. The lift starts to move up the floors, and my brother studies me for a moment.

"You're reading short-term intentions now," he comments. "But, like, well before they act on them."

"Yeah." I shrug. "I guess I am."

Before Blair, before the bond, I could read intentions, but it was more long-term, overall intention. Now, I'm starting to read short-term ones, even when they're impulsive. And more than that, the intentions are becoming clearer. The bond is strengthening me.

The elevator continues its climb toward the sky.

Thirty floors.

Forty floors.

The fear spikes again as we pass the fiftieth floor, but it's not my fear. It's *hers*. And the closer I get to her, the more I can feel her. The more I can sense her.

Fuck, I need to get to her!

My hands curl into fists as the cart comes to a stop on the

sixtieth floor. The elevator dings softly, announcing our arrival to whoever is on the other side of the door, and both Cal and I brace ourselves for what's to come.

The door slides open, and we both step out to find two guards—gofers again—standing in the private hallway outside the penthouse.

Both spot us, and the first dude's intention, the one with the dark hair, hits me like lightning.

Kill.

I cross the distance before his hand can finish the path to his gun, snapping his head sideways with a sharp crack. He drops instantly.

The second dude barely manages to clear his weapon before Cal dives onto him, taking him to the floor and wrapping both of his hands around his neck until he strangles the life out of him.

Instantly, silence fills the hallway, and we keep moving, stepping over the bodies, and don't stop until we reach the front door of Damien's penthouse.

I attempt to open the door, but when Cal notices a card swipe above the lock, he jogs back to one of the dead guards, checking his pockets until he finds what we need.

A minute after that, we're swiping the gofer's keycard and entering Damien Snow's penthouse. It's fancy as fuck, and the entrance hallway is no doubt bigger than our living room at the cabin.

But just before we reach the end of the long foyer, Damien Snow steps into view. His eyes narrow when our gazes meet.

"Who the fuck are you?"

"We're the men who killed your two gofers outside."

"You have got to be fucking kidding me," he hisses at me. "You're those fucking Slater brother fucks, aren't you?"

"Pretty sure no one's joking, fucker."

"Do you have any idea whose building you're standing in?" He snarls. "Do you have any clue who you're messing with right now? Do you have fucking sense at all? The Elite Council wants your heads on a silver platter."

When Cal starts to react, starts to step forward, I put my hand on his chest. *If anyone is killing this motherfucker, it's me.*

"They find out about this little preselection scheme you evidently have going with Holland, and they're going to want your head too, dickhead. The only difference is that that'll scare you. You cow to the Council. We spit in their faces. We don't give a fuck. We're here for her," I say. "Let her fucking go."

"Oh wow." He laughs at that. "So, you think you can come in here and demand shit? Blackmail me as if the Council would believe anything you fucks have to say? That's rich."

"And you think you can be a disgusting, vile piece of shit and get away with it?" I mock. "Not on my watch, motherfucker."

"This is going to be a nice day for me," he says, lips curling in a devious smile. "First, I'm going to kill you. And then, I'm going to breed her and drain her. Hell, maybe I'll just fucking drain her instead, just to spite you. Watch the light go right out of her eyes while I drink every drop of her blood."

Rage flows through me like a river. I will *murder* him. "You will not lay a fucking finger on her."

His intention hits me full force. It's sharp and violent, and it whispers six words, *Kill him and then kill her.*

Before he can even lift a hand, before he can reach for the

gun I know is in his jacket pocket, I shove all my fucking rage toward him and his arm freezes in midair. His eyes go wide, and I close the distance between us from the other end of the corridor in the blink of an eye.

"You—" Damien starts, but the word never finishes because I have one hand already wrapped around his throat, lifting him off his fucking feet.

I add my second hand to his neck and twist. Hard. The crack is sharp and precise, but I don't stop after that. I don't stop when his body goes lifeless beneath my fingers. I don't stop until I've twisted so hard and with so much force that his body drops to the floor while his head still rests between my fucking palms.

Silence fills the corridor again.

"Well," Cal says calmly behind me. "The numbers are climbing."

I let Damien's head drop unceremoniously to the floor, and it hits the marble with a thud.

But I'm no longer focused on Damien or Cal; I'm looking at the door beside me.

Because I know, on the other side, is *Blair.*

28

A SOB ESCAPES MY CHEST, AND I BURY MY FACE into my Kane doll's hair.

But when a harsh sound cuts through the room, I freeze.

I hear another loud noise echo through the penthouse, and my heart starts pounding wildly in my chest.

Footsteps are outside the door, and I stare at it in anticipation, fully expecting Damien to come back inside and grow angry that I didn't follow his instructions.

My mind races, my heart beats against my rib cage, and I make a concerted effort to hide the doll under the bed while I stare at the door, bracing myself for whatever is going to happen next.

For a second, nothing happens.

And then the lock clicks.

It's such a small sound, but it might as well be a gunshot.

I stare at the handle, and it twists violently before the steel door explodes inward. The hinges scream as the door tears open so hard it slams against the wall.

And then Kane is standing there, his eyes wild as he scans the room.

For a moment, I can't breathe.

He looks godlike as his large frame fills the doorway—his broad shoulders, his dark clothes, his thick muscles beneath his jeans and T-shirt. And then his gaze meets mine. His eyes are filled with an intensity that makes my entire world narrow to him and only him.

Kane. He's here. In New York. In this room.

My brain tries to make sense of it, but my body moves before the thought finishes forming. Without hesitation or fear or doubt, I run straight to him.

For a split second, I'm terrified he'll disappear—that I imagined him, that this is just another trick my mind is playing after everything that's happened.

But he doesn't disappear. He meets me halfway.

His hands close around my arms, and he pulls me to a stop, his eyes moving quickly over my face, my neck, my shoulders. His gaze travels down my arms, my waist, my legs.

"Did he hurt you?" The question comes out rough. "Did he fucking touch you?"

"No." My voice breaks as the tears spill faster. My whole body is shaking. "No."

And the moment the word leaves my mouth, something in him shifts.

His arms come around me instantly, pulling me tight against his chest, and a flow of tears starts up again, streaming down my face as I bury my face into his shirt and breathe him in.

The relief is overwhelming, consuming every nerve ending

in my body, and I fist my hands in the front of his shirt. My hands shake and my knees tremble and the panic that's been clawing at my chest since Damien locked the door is gone. Completely gone.

Kane's here. He's really here.

"I'm sorry," I sob into his shoulder. "I'm so sorry."

He pulls back just enough to look at me, one finger sliding gently beneath my chin so I have to meet his eyes. "It's okay, Blair."

"You were right about everything," I whisper. "I just…I couldn't wrap my head around it. It was so hard to—"

"I know," he murmurs softly. "I know, baby. It's okay. I've got you."

Then his mouth is on mine. The kiss is deep and urgent, and I taste the salt of my tears between us. His hand cradles the back of my head like he's afraid to let me go.

"You came," I whisper against his lips.

His forehead presses against mine. "I always will."

My chest tightens as the question I've been holding finally spills out. "How did you even find me? How did you know?"

His eyes turn tender as he looks at me. "I would've found you anywhere, Blair," he says quietly. "I belong to you. You belong to me. We're fate, baby. We're fucking fate."

The words hit something deep inside me—something I stopped fighting the moment I saw him standing in that doorway.

"I love you," I say, my voice trembling. "I don't even know why… But I do, Kane. I love you."

He cups my face. "I love you too."

The fear that's been choking me since Damien locked that door finally loosens its grip.

"I want to go home," I say softly.

But the place that comes to mind isn't my parents' mansion in Boston.

"I want to go back to the cabin."

Kane brushes his thumb gently across my cheek, wiping away the last of my tears. "Let's go home."

29

KANE

CAL AND I MADE QUICK WORK OF LEAVING DAMIEN'S penthouse and getting back to the cabin. We used our vampire speed and ran, and I carried Blair the whole way, refusing to let go of her until we made it safely home. And Cal kept his eyes and ears fixated on any threats or gofer fucks following our trail as we ran.

Rook was grateful when we walked through the door. Kylie, too. But I simply couldn't hang around for a chitchat. I carried Blair straight to our bedroom—yes, *our* fucking bedroom—and shut the door behind us.

The cabin is quiet for the most part. Rook and Kylie and Cal are all chatting quietly downstairs, and the occasional wind blows through the trees. It's the kind of quiet that only exists this deep in the woods.

But none of that reaches me. All I'm aware of is Blair.

She's in my room, in my bed, and in my arms. Her mouth is on mine, desperate in a way like she's been holding back for way too long. Her hands slide up my chest, fingers curling into my shirt before pushing it over my shoulders.

"Kane," she whispers my name against my lips, and fuck, do I love the sound of it.

I kiss her again, slower this time, grounding myself in the warmth of her body pressed against mine. Her hands move to the hem of her own shirt, working it over her head with quick, frantic movements.

A soft laugh leaves my lips as I reach up to catch her wrists gently. "Slow down."

She blinks up at me. "Why?"

Because if she keeps moving like this, I won't stop. Because I've wanted this since the moment I saw her. Because every instinct in my body says she's already mine.

But that's exactly why I force myself to take a step back.

"You deserve to know what this means," I tell her.

Her brow furrows slightly, but she doesn't pull away. "I already know what it means," she says softly.

"No," I say quietly. "You know what it feels like. That's not the same thing."

Her eyes search mine, and I brush my thumb along her jaw.

"We're fated mates, Blair."

The words settle between us.

"You said that before," she whispers.

"I did. And it's not just some romantic phrase, baby. It's a bond. Once it's sealed, it's permanent."

Her breath catches. "Permanent how?"

"There's no walking away from it," I say. "No undoing it. No pretending it didn't happen. We'll be connected forever. We'll be together forever." My hand moves to the back of her neck, holding her there gently. "You and I will basically be one, baby. No takebacks. No detours. It'll be you and me for life. And you'll live a long life, at that. Much longer than a normal human would."

Her lips part like she's about to say something, but I do my best to make sure she understands what a fated mate bond truly means. That she knows what she's signing up for if she gives me all of herself.

"I know you're a virgin, baby," I whisper. "And that's why this will be such a powerful thing. It's why if we cross that line tonight, you and I will be bound. Completely."

She studies my face for a moment, but then something softens in her expression. "I've tried to fight this since the moment you took me," she says quietly. Her fingers slide up my chest again, resting over my heart. "But I can't." She takes a slow breath. "I'm always thinking about you," she admits, and her words hit me square in the chest.

But she keeps going. "I always want to be near you. Even when I was angry at you, even when I thought you were some crazy psycho who ruined my life… I still wanted you close. I still only felt safe when I was by your side."

Her eyes shine in the dim light of the room.

"Kane, when you're not there, it feels wrong. Like something's missing. Like I'm only half a person. And when you touch me…" she continues softly, "everything else…stops. I just want you. I only want you."

For a second, I can't speak. Every word she just said echoes something inside me that I've been carrying alone. She's giving me everything I've been desperate for, and I honestly wasn't sure if I would ever get anything from her.

I wasn't sure if she'd hate me forever.

"The moment I laid eyes on you, my entire fucking world shifted. Like everything I was before suddenly had a direction. Like you were my compass and purpose and home." I brush my knuckles along her cheek. "It's why I took you."

Her breath catches.

"It's why I killed for you."

Her hand tightens against my chest.

"And it's why I'll do anything for you."

The room goes still.

"You're mine. And I'm yours. And if we take the next step..." I pause, making sure she hears every word. "...there's no going back."

She studies me for a long moment.

Then she moves closer.

She slides her hands up my chest and around my neck. "I don't want to go back," she whispers, and then she brushes her lips against mine. "I want you."

Our connection surges between us, and my restraint cracks.

I pull her back into my arms and kiss her deeply, my hands sliding along her waist as she melts against me.

Every instinct in my body recognizes her.

Mine.

And when she whispers my name again against my lips, I know neither of us is turning back now.

30

I'VE NEVER SEEN A MORE BEAUTIFUL SIGHT THAN Kane naked. His thick muscles look corded as they flex to remove the rest of my clothes, and his big, hard cock juts out from his body like it's already trying to find a way inside me.

Goodness, I want him inside me.

I haven't showered. I still have mud on my body, but I don't fucking care. I just need him. I need him so badly that my entire body aches.

A little moan leaves my lips when he spreads my thighs and kneels between them. His gaze is fixated on my exposed flesh, where I'm already waiting and throbbing for him, and he licks his lips.

"God, you're beautiful, Blair. So fucking beautiful."

Another moan escapes my lips as he leans forward to just barely graze his lips over my pussy. My hips jolt forward, like my body is trying to find its way to his mouth, and I don't miss the little smile that crosses his mouth.

"I'm going to savor this. I'm going to taste and tease and lick and suck every inch of you."

At his words alone, my pussy clenches.

And before I even have to beg, his mouth is on me, sucking and licking and eating at me in a way I've never experienced in my life. Pleasure rolls through my body in tight waves, and my moans grow more intense as his mouth devours me.

"You taste so fucking good." He moans against my skin. "I swear, I'm going to spend the rest of my life eating you. It's all I need to survive."

He reaches up with his big hands to palm my breasts, and my breaths turn into erratic pants as he continues to push me closer and closer to the edge.

When my climax starts to form at the base of my spine, I try to push him away. "No. Please. I want you inside me," I beg.

But he just looks up at me through hooded, heated eyes and grins.

"Oh Blair, but this isn't going to be your only orgasm tonight."

And then he puts his mouth back on me, his hands moving to my thighs to spread them as wide as they can go, and he licks and sucks at my clit until I can't keep the waves of euphoria at bay. I come so hard stars dance behind my eyes, and sounds I don't even understand escape my lungs.

But he doesn't stop.

He just keeps eating at me. Licking at me. Devouring me until I come again.

And just when I think he's done, he flips me over onto my belly and buries his face against me again, licking my pussy and my ass like he can't get enough of me.

I've never experienced a man touching me like this, kissing me like this. I've never experienced anything like this in my entire life, and I swear on everything, I feel like the luckiest girl in the world, and he hasn't even put his cock inside me yet.

When he brings me to another orgasm, I actually scream.

I don't know my name by the time he flips me back over, his mouth and cheeks covered in my arousal. He's still kneeling between my thighs, smiling down at me, as he starts to stroke his very hard cock with his hand.

"You're mine."

I nod. "I'm yours."

"Say it again."

"I'm yours, Kane. Forever. For always."

He reaches out to grip my thighs again, spreading them out as he slowly starts to slide his cock inside me. I'm so wet by now he slides in easily, but the pleasurable pain that comes from being filled for the first time makes my eyes fall shut and a moan escape my lips.

He feels huge as he slides his cock into me inch by inch, and I don't think I've ever felt more complete in my entire life as when I do when my body is this full of him.

And he sits there for a long moment, his gaze locked with mine.

"This is heaven," he whispers. "This is fucking heaven."

"Yes. More. I need more." I wiggle my hips a little, encouraging him to move, and he doesn't hesitate to pull back slightly before driving his hips forward.

And then he does it again.

And again.

And again.

Each thrust going deep and harder and my breasts bouncing from the movement.

More moans spill from my lips, but I don't miss the way his gaze moves to my neck, watching the way it pulses with each beat of my heart.

"I know what you are, Kane." Without hesitation, I reach out to pull his face closer to mine. "And I know what feeding is. I know what it is, and I want it. I want you to feed on me."

His gaze sharpens. "You shouldn't say that lightly."

"I'm not."

My pulse is already quickening, but it isn't fear that drives it. It's anticipation. It's desire. It's need. I want him to feed on me. I want it so badly, I actually feel physical pain from it.

"I want you to feed on me. I know what it means. I know what it does. And I just…I need that connection with you more than I need anything else." I reach up and touch the side of his neck, feeling the tension in him. "I need it, Kane. Please. Feed on me."

He stills. "Blair—"

"Please," I beg. "Please." I take his hand and guide it to my heart. "You feel that? That's what you do to me," I whisper, sliding his hand along my throat. "And I know what I want."

His jaw clenches with restraint. "You're asking me to lose complete control."

"I trust you, Kane. And when you're with me like this, I want you to be reckless. I want you to be wild. I want you to give me everything because I want to give you everything too."

His cock is still deep inside me, and I move my hips a little just to savor the feel of him filling me. He groans and starts driving his cock in again.

"Be wild with me," I plead, and I see when the last vestige of his restraint leaves his body.

He fucks me hard and fast, and then he pauses as he leans down to brush his lips against my neck. "I'm going to fuck you while I feed on you. And I'm going to feed on you while I make you come on my cock."

And when his mouth moves slowly down my throat, his lips warm against my skin, I know I was right. The beast in him isn't something to fear.

It's something I want. It's something I need.

It's something I'll crave forever.

31

KANE

THE MOMENT BLAIR TILTS HER HEAD AND OFFERS me her throat, I snap. I lose control. I let myself inhale her, taking in the scent of her blood. Her pulse flutters beneath my mouth—fast, warm, and so beautifully alive.

My mouth waters, my cock jerks inside her, and I reach up with my hand to wrap my fingers gently around her neck.

She smells like fucking heaven.

She smells like *mine*.

"Last chance," I murmur against her skin. "Tell me to stop."

"Don't you dare." She tightens her fingers on my shoulders, digging her nails into my skin hard enough to draw blood if I were human.

A dark sound leaves my chest. "You have no idea what you're asking for."

She lifts her chin higher, exposing her throat fully now and ensuring that my lips brush against her skin. "I do," she whispers. "Be wild with me."

That's it. That's the moment the beast inside me stops pretending to be civilized. I slide my hand behind her neck and hold her there as my mouth brushes the racing pulse beneath her skin. I feel the tremor that runs through her body, and her intentions roll over me like a tidal wave.

There's no fear. Just anticipation. Just desire. Just need.

She wants this as much as I do.

She needs, in fact. Just like I need it. Just like I need her.

I sink my teeth into her skin, the bite quick and precise, and the instant her blood touches my tongue, my entire world fractures.

Heat floods through me like lightning under my skin. The taste of her is richer than anything I've ever known—warm and alive in a way that feels sacred.

Mine.

Electricity pulses through me, and I thrust my cock inside her as I suck at her throat, taking drop after drop of her blood.

It feels like an invisible thread knots itself between my heart and hers. Like we'll forever be connected now, in life and in death. Like our entire beings will find a way to be together for eternity.

Blair gasps softly against my shoulder, her body arching toward mine as the connection deepens. And I feed on her while I keep her pussy stuffed full of my cock.

I can feel her emotions as clearly as my own now—desire, trust, and the fierce certainty that she chose this. That she chose me.

That realization would bring me to my knees if I were standing, but it makes me drive my cock deep inside her and stay there while I slide my teeth out of her neck, licking the mark closed as I tighten my arms around her.

Her breathing is shaky, but she slides her hands into my hair, pulling my face back to hers.

Her eyes are bright and wild.

"I can feel that you chose me," she whispers. "I can feel that you love me. I can feel that you're certain about me. I can feel everything you're feeling."

Every cell in my body hums from her admission. "It's the bond. It's destiny. It's you and me."

"Fated mates," she whispers.

"I love you."

"I love you too, Kane."

She kisses me again, and the bond burns and pulses between us, while every touch is amplified until even the smallest movement feels electric.

"I want everything with you," she whispers against my mouth. "I want forever. I want the present and the future. I want you to fill me with your come. I want you to fill my belly with your babies."

I want nothing more than to breed her. I want nothing more than to fill her up with every drop of come inside my cock.

And that's exactly what I do.

I drive my cock in and out of her, feeling her tight pussy clench around me until she grips me like a vise. Until moans spill from her lips and her eyes fall closed.

Until I push myself as deep as I can go and come deep inside her.

My Blair. My mate. *Fucking mine.*

32

SUNRISE AT THE CABIN IS MY FAVORITE TIME OF day. The mountains turn gold first. Then the trees. Then the lake off in the distance catches the light, and everything looks like it's glowing.

I lean against the railing of the deck, wrapping my sweater a little tighter around myself as the cool morning air brushes my skin.

The old Blair would've been disgusted by this place—*was* disgusted by this place. That girl thought her future looked like penthouses and wealth and private flights on private jets and luxury shopping sprees.

She would've—*did*—snubbed her nose at a rustic cabin in the woods with three blue-collar vampire brothers and a human girl who used to work at an accounting firm.

But I'm not that girl anymore. I'm different. I'm happy. I'm grateful. *I'm Kane's.*

Now, this cabin feels like peace. Now, it feels like home.

It's only been a few days since Kane saved me from Damien's apartment and we sealed our fated mates' bond. But I feel like I've known him all my life. Honestly, I think I have; it just took me a little bit to realize it.

He *is* my doll—the man I spent my childhood waiting for—but better. My heart has always been waiting for him to come save me, and even as I fought it, he did.

That first night he saved me from Damien—and after we'd made love for the first time—Kane asked me about my doll while I was rummaging through my suitcase I thought I'd never get back. I told him all the lore of a young Blair Windsor getting a set of vampire dolls for her birthday, but the one with the green-violet eyes and light-colored hair was her favorite.

And I told him how the first time I laid eyes on him, he reminded me of it.

Now, every morning when Kane makes the bed, he finishes it off by propping my vampire doll on our pillows. It's pretty damn cute, to be honest.

I know in my bones that I am where I'm supposed to be. Sure, there's currently a lot of danger to watch out for related to the elite. And I know the future isn't certain and there are things I still need to figure out related to my family and my old life, but I wouldn't trade life with Kane for anything.

Old Blair would be appalled that this life doesn't include Damien Snow's penthouse or the elites or wealth, but she was too naïve for her own good.

She didn't understand what real power was, what real love was.

But because of Kane, I know better.

I glance over my shoulder toward our bedroom window, and instantly, I think about how he already made love to me three times this morning and still looked like he wanted to carry me back to bed when I slipped out quietly while he took a shower.

My cheeks warm. *Three orgasms and the sun had barely come up.*

Unconsciously, my hand drifts to my stomach. *Goodness.* The fact that a small, hopeful part of me already wonders if I might get pregnant with Kane's babies soon is…honestly ridiculous.

A month ago, I thought I needed someone rich and powerful.

Instead, I found someone whose real power is doing good. Someone protective. Someone who puts me first always. Someone who makes me laugh—which is another thing I didn't know I needed in a man, but I do.

Someone who does what's right, even when it's hard.

And he's not alone in these qualities; his brothers have them too.

When it comes to the Slater brothers, Cal is the quiet one, but every once in a while, he'll say something so dry and perfectly timed that I lose it.

Rook is grumpy ninety percent of the time…but somehow still funny.

But Kane? *God help me.* That man is the biggest jokester of them all. I don't think I've laughed so much in my life as I have the past forty-eight hours we've been attached at the hip.

And the three of them together spend most of their time trying to help women who don't know they need it.

I hear the door behind me open.

Speak of the handsome devil.

"Thought maybe you tried to escape again," Kane teases, and I glance over my shoulder to find him leaning in the doorway. He's shirtless, and his blond hair is still a little damp from his shower. And his mouth is etched in a smile that has him looking entirely too pleased with himself for this early in the morning.

God, I love him.

"You're the one who doesn't sleep," I point out. "I figured you'd still be upstairs plotting how to seduce me again."

"Plotting?" His grin widens. "Pretty sure all I need to do is put my mouth on your pussy and we're all set."

"Shut up." I giggle and blush and stick out my tongue at him.

He winks at me before pushing himself off the doorway and closing the distance between us. I expect him to pinch my butt or plant a big ol' kiss on my lips, but he just wraps his arm around my waist instead.

"Love you, baby."

I tilt my head up to press a kiss to his jaw. "Love you too."

"I have something for you."

My curiosity sparks instantly. "What?"

He grips my hips and turns me toward him. "I figured out a way for you to see your family."

"What?" My breath catches. "Really?"

"Yes. Your mom, your dad, and Bonnie, too."

"How?" I ask quietly.

"Cal helped me work out the logistics."

Cal has this terrifying ability to hear things from miles away if he concentrates. Which means he's been listening to elite conversations, tracking information, and piecing together movements.

"But you said they still think I'm in New York. With Damien," I say slowly.

Kane nods. "And they're still sticking with that story. Your parents very much think Damien is alive and well and you're happy with him and that he plans to choose you at the *Choosing Ceremony*," he says the last two words in jest.

Because it's not a Choosing Ceremony. It's a fucking auction. One that hasn't happened yet but will be happening soon.

Not only are the elites actively trying to find Kane and his brothers and Kylie and me, but they're keeping everything quiet—aka straight-up lying—when it comes to my parents.

Which means my parents are just…living their lives and completely unaware of the truth.

Kane presses a kiss to my forehead. "We're going to meet them today."

"Today?" My heart jumps. "Where? How?"

"A park outside Boston. Near a nature trail. It's very private."

I search his eyes. "But is it safe?"

"Yes," he says. "I mean, it's a little bit of a risk, but I know it's something you have to do. And Cal and Rook and Kylie all support it. But we only have a short window," he continues. "So, we have to go now."

Emotion rushes through me so suddenly I move without thinking, but before I make it all the way to the door, I skid to a stop and run back to him.

Immediately, I grab his face and kiss him hard.

"I love you," I say between erratic kisses all over his face. "I love you…I love you…I love you… Thank you!"

He laughs softly against my lips. "You're welcome."

But when I pull back, I study him. "Are you really sure this is okay?"

Because this isn't small. The elites want us all dead. So I know that moving around this close to Boston isn't without danger.

Kane brushes his thumb along my cheek. "Go get dressed, Blair." He kisses my forehead again. "We don't have much time."

I grin and spin on my heels, and he manages to sneak a butt smack in before I get to the door.

"Move it, baby!"

"Rude!" I squeal and run toward the door.

"Hey, Blair?"

"Yeah?"

"If you take longer than ten minutes, I'm coming upstairs." And the heated, playful, downright obscene look in his eyes says he means it.

Which I can't deny is tempting as hell, but…*I get to see my family today.*

"I'm going! I'm going! Keep your pants on!" I laugh and run inside.

Technically, it took me fifteen minutes to get ready, but that's because I actually have clothes that fit me now. Yesterday, I demanded Kane get me things—additional makeup, hair and skin products, new clothes. You know, normal human girl stuff.

He only acted annoyed for a good thirty seconds, but then he simply found a way to make all my materialistic dreams come true, and he came back to the cabin with bags in his hands filled with all the things I wanted.

I might not be Old Blair anymore, but I still have priorities, you know?

We couldn't travel by car—that'd be too easy to track—so we traveled by foot the whole way with me on Kane's back and Cal following closely behind. Now, we're just outside of Boston in a quiet little park in a quiet little suburb you wouldn't even know existed if someone didn't tell you about it.

Just as we reach the tree line, Kane sets me on my feet. But when I try to hold his hand, he shakes his head. "I'll be here," he says. "You go."

I scrunch up my nose and search his face closely.

"If you need me, I'll be right here."

"Are you sure?"

He doesn't need to answer me—I can feel his intention. I can feel his response.

He wants to give me space—but not too much space. He wants to protect me and watch over me and keep me safe. But he also wants to give me room to see my family and feel out the conversation and how they react.

We don't have certainty about what they know or don't know. I have no idea if my dad knows the truth about the elites or if my mom understands what a Choosing Ceremony actually stands for.

I have so many questions, and I need so many answers. But mostly, I just want to see them. I want to hug them. And I want them to see that I'm okay.

But before I try to look for them, I walk back to Kane and stand up on my tippy-toes to press a kiss to his lips. "I love you."

"I love you too, baby."

And then, I turn back on my heel and walk toward the park.

It doesn't take me long to find them; my mom and dad stand beside a wooden park bench that Bonnie's parked her cute butt on. She's staring down at her phone, but my parents are very much looking around the park.

It takes them another ten seconds before they spot me.

But then they do.

"Blair!" my mom calls toward me, waving both hands in the air as a giant smile consumes her face.

Bonnie looks up from her phone, and a huge, relieved smile spreads across her lips. And my dad's reaction is very much the same.

I quickly close the distance between us, and my mom doesn't hesitate to pull me into a tight hug. "Oh my God, I've missed you," she says just as my dad wraps his arms around both of us.

"Good to see you, sweetheart," he says.

"God, my family is truly embarrassing," Bonnie mutters, but then, on a snort, she doesn't hesitate to add herself to our hug.

I laugh through the sudden sting of tears. "I missed you guys."

"Are you okay?" My mom pulls back to study my face. "And… oh my…what are you wearing?" she asks, her gaze moving down my simple T-shirt and jeans and sneakers.

"Yes, I'm okay," I answer. "And I've been going a little more casual these days."

She pinches her mouth into a firm line, but she doesn't say anything else about my wardrobe. Honestly, it's a surprise. "Damien told us you got to New York safely, but you've been impossible to reach," she says in a rush. "I had to call Holland to give me updates. He said everything was good but Damien has been keeping you very busy. Lots of traveling to very fancy places." She smiles, and my stomach drops. "I can't wait to hear all about it."

I had no idea how this was going to go, and Cal has been able to get enough information during his surveillance trips for me to know my parents appeared in the dark. I honestly thought I was prepared, but it's a whole different story when I have to face their naïveté head on.

I search both of their faces, taking in the way their eyes are unguarded and their shoulders are relaxed. And my mother. Goodness. She's downright giddy right now.

A woman who knows the truth about Damien, about the elites, about the auction, wouldn't look like this.

And my dad is very much the same.

I've racked my brain, wondering if I were some kind of pawn in my parents' game with the elites, but it's clear to me that I wasn't the pawn at all. They were the pawns. The elites told them all the things they wanted to hear, and none of those things was the truth.

Now it makes sense why my father's great-aunt Estelle hardly kept in contact with anyone in her family after she attended a Choosing Ceremony decades ago and found her vampire "husband." Now it makes sense why she ended up in "Rome."

I shudder to think what actually happened to her.

"Oh, come on, Blair!" My mom practically squeals. "Don't leave me hanging! Tell me how things are with Damien! Tell me where you've been and what you've been up to! It's really sounding like he's going to choose you at the ceremony."

Oh boy. I don't even know what to say. I don't know what to do. On the one hand, I want to tell them the truth. But on the other hand, I don't know what consequences the truth would have for them. It's clear the elites are making a big effort to keep them in the dark, even though I have no idea why.

So, I do the only thing I can do right now. I put on a fake smile and pretend that everything is what they think it is. "How much time do you have?" I tease, forcing a laugh from my throat. "Things have been good. Just very, very busy."

"We have loads of time!" She nudges me playfully. "Tell us everything. Tell me—"

"Oh, come on, Devney," my dad cuts her off on a laugh. "Give our daughter a little room to breathe before you start interrogating her."

She gently slaps my dad on the shoulder. "Mind your business."

He just laughs, but when he glances past me for a brief moment, he tilts his head to the side. "Does he work for Damien?"

I look over my shoulder to follow his gaze, and immediately, I spot Kane standing calmly near the tree line. He's right where he said he'd be.

Our eyes meet, and something passes between us. It's not words but understanding and silent communication. I know his ears can hear every word, and I know he's well aware of my father's question.

I want them to know who Kane is to me. I want them to know the truth—that Kane saved my life, that the elites wanted to destroy me. I want them to meet the love of my life. But I fear the truth won't set them free.

I fear the truth will become a noose around their necks.

I fear the truth will put them in danger.

Instantly, I can feel his response. *He agrees. He thinks it's better that way. All of his intentions are pure and focused on keeping not just me safe, but my family too.*

He wants to protect them as well.

And so do I because my parents don't need to be dragged into this, and Bonnie is far too young for this world.

Maybe someday the truth will surface. Maybe someday my father will hear whispers that Damien Snow is dead.

But not today. Today, I protect them.

"Yeah," I say lightly, answering my father's question. "Damien has someone keeping an eye on me."

"That's good." My mom nods and smiles. "Things in New York can be…dangerous."

Oh Mom, you have no idea.

Eventually, the four of us walk the short trail together. We talk about small things. Normal life things. Bonnie tells me about her annoying English teacher and that she broke up with Josh for the fourth time.

My mom updates me on the upcoming charity event she's planning to raise funds for cancer research.

My dad talks about some business deal he landed that will help him expand his company into the Asian market.

They tell me about this new Italian restaurant they found near their house and make me promise to have dinner with them soon.

And the entire time, I memorize everything—their voices, their faces, and the sounds of my little sister's laughter.

Because I don't know when I'll see them again.

Right now, things are too dangerous.

Right now, I need to stick to Kane and the cabin.

When we make it back to the park bench I found them near, Kane steps forward just enough to grab my attention. *It's time to go.*

My chest tightens, but I don't hesitate to give my mom and dad and Bonnie a hug. "I need to head out."

"Let me guess," my mother says, giving me an extra squeeze, "Damien probably has something special planned for you."

I smile. "Something like that."

"Call us next time you're free, sweetheart."

"I will."

My dad kisses the top of my head. "Stay safe."

Bonnie squeezes me one last time. "Love you."

"Love you too," I tell her, but when she tries to end the hug, I pull her closer to me. "You were right to be suspicious," I whisper low and directly into her ear. "But I'm safe, okay? I'm safe. Just don't ever let them talk you into being chosen."

I lean back and meet her eyes. She searches my face and then pulls me into another hug. Her breath is hot as she whispers at my ear. "The guy who works for Damien looks an awful lot like your doll."

I nod, my chin digging into her shoulder. "Yes. He does."

When I pull back again, she offers a sage nod and reaches out to squeeze my hand one last time before I walk away. She's smarter than me. She gets it now—without needing to be kidnapped or dragged through the same brutal convincing I was—there's much more to the vampire world than our parents told us.

There's more to the vampire world than either of us ever dreamed.

I can't deny that leaving my family behind is hard, but it

doesn't even come close to what it felt like to be stuck in Damien's penthouse, thinking I would never see Kane again.

I cross the clearing toward him, and once we're out of sight, once we're away from the park, he pauses to wrap his arms around me and hold me tight against his chest.

"You okay?" he whispers into my ear, and I nod.

Because I am.

I'm more than okay.

I'm whole. I'm alive. I'm *his*.

33

KANE

B LAIR SITS CURLED ON THE COUCH BESIDE KYLIE, their heads bent together while they talk about something that makes them both laugh. The sound fills the room in a way I didn't realize this place had been missing before. *Peace. Actual fucking peace.*

Cal sits at the kitchen table, messing around with brake calipers from an old timer that lives in the shed. And Rook leans against the far wall with his arms crossed, pretending not to listen but smirking anyway. Even my older, usually broody-as-fuck brother looks relaxed.

The day went better than any of us expected.

Blair saw her family without the elites catching wind, and I got her back to the cabin safely.

The bond between us hums softly in my chest now. It's steady, it's strong, and I know with certainty she's mine.

I glance over at her, and when she catches me looking, she playfully rolls her eyes. She also smiles too.

My woman is a stubborn, strong-willed firecracker, and I fucking love her.

I'm about to walk over to her sassy ass, throw her over my shoulder, and take her to bed, but before I get three steps across the living room, I pause when I hear a knock at the door.

The sound lands hard against the cabin door, and everyone in the room freezes.

Rook lifts his head.

Cal stands.

And I head straight for the door.

No one knocks out here. *Ever.*

A second knock follows the first, but this one is slow in a way that feels *intentional.*

My instincts flare, all my senses focused on what's on the other side of the door. But all my ears pick up is *one* set of footsteps.

I glance over my shoulder to make sure Blair is still on the couch with Kylie, and when her eyes meet mine, I see concern etched on her face.

Without hesitation, Rook and Cal step closer to the door with me. We don't even talk about it.

We move, silently communicating to one another without words, the entire time ensuring we're a shield to the women behind us.

All three of us know there's no avoiding it. All three of us know the only option is to open the door.

Rook swings it open, and we come face-to-face with an older vampire who currently occupies the threshold of our front door.

He's tall, dressed to showcase money, and his hair is pepper gray. He's calm as his glowing green eyes look at all three of us.

For some reason, I recognize him, and it doesn't take long for a memory to click into place. *The preview event. The night I found Blair. He was there.*

He's elite.

"Hello, Rook. Kane." His smile deepens as his eyes slide across all three of us. "Calloway."

"Who the fuck are you?" Rook asks without hesitation.

The man laughs, a full, amused belly laugh that vibrates his chest. "Lucian," he declares. "Lucian Wrath. Vice President of the Elite Council."

Oh fuck. They found us.

Something strange flickers across Lucian's face. It's not hostility, but it's not approval either. It's something else. And fuck does it have me on edge.

I already know he's a shield just like Holland. I can tell by the way his brain has created a steel fortress that I can't break through to read his intentions. I'm sure Rook is in the same boat, telepathy not an option at all.

"I've been waiting for this moment," Lucian says, and the words hang heavy in the night air.

His gaze flicks toward the inside of the cabin briefly before moving back to us.

"And I knew you three would be the ones to change things."

The night suddenly feels different. The world shifts. And the peace I was feeling before has been replaced by the kind of uncertainty that makes you feel like you're standing on the edge of a cliff, ready to dive into the unknown.

Lucian Wrath simply smiles, as if he already knows how this story will unfold.

But I don't have a fucking clue what's going to happen next.

With two fingers to his lips, Lucian lets out a low whistle from his mouth. The sound barely leaves his throat before the night explodes into chaos.

Men in black cars screech to a stop in the driveway, and eight, ten, maybe fifteen fucking vampires move more quickly than we can react to surround the house.

This war we started is in full swing.

The men we've killed demand to be avenged. The women we've taken—though bound to Slaters by the universe's decree—the elites believe were promised to them.

And by their code, we owe them our heads.

This isn't the end yet…
Read *Demolition Man* today!
(The next and final book in the
Blue-Collar Vigilante Vampire Series)

**You know you want to read Calloway Slater's book…
Read Demolition Man today!**
This is the next and final book in the highly addictive
Blue-Collar Vigilante Vampire Series!
Check out the entire series here:
Blue-Collar Vigilante Vampires
https://geni.us/BCVV_Series

Sign up for our newsletter, and we'll keep you up-to-date on
any **exciting vigilante vampire** news, AND a lot of times, we
share fun teasers and excerpts for our upcoming releases!
www.authormaxmonroe.com/newsletter

Need EVEN MORE Max Monroe?
Check out our Suggested Reading Order on our website!
www.authormaxmonroe.com/max-monroe-suggested-reading-order

Follow us online here:
Facebook: www.facebook.com/authormaxmonroe
Reader Group: www.facebook.com/
groups/1561640154166388
Twitter: www.twitter.com/authormaxmonroe
Instagram: www.instagram.com/authormaxmonroe
TikTok:_vm.tiktok.com/ZMe1jv5kQ/
Goodreads: https://goo.gl/8VUIz2

Acknowledgments

To all the most important people in our lives.

You know who you are.

We couldn't do this without you.

We love you.

To all our reader friends, THANK YOU FOR READING. You're the best.

And last, but certainly not least, to our dream team. The people who surround us and help us turn our words into books. The people who help us reach our readers. The people who support us every step of the way in this industry. Mark Gottlieb, Lisa Hollett, Stacey Blake, Kim Greene, Rick Hambright, Peter Alderweireld, Joanne Cote-Felaccio, Kristina Hassaker, and so many more amazing people, we are forever grateful for you.

XOXO,
Max & Monroe

www.ingramcontent.com/pod-product-compliance
Lightning Source LLC
Chambersburg PA
CBHW030900060726
47591CB00005B/1362